Within These Woods

CASSIE HOPWOOD

Cassie Hopwood

For all of my fellow Halloween freaks

For my dad, who gave me the incredible experience of working in a haunted house and so many of the ideas I had for this story

And most importantly, for God, who has carried me through life and shown me both the good and the bad side of our world

WITHIN THESE WOODS

~ 1 ~

METSAH

There is a memory that sticks out in my mind like no other. It haunts me as a terrifying, other-worldly experience, but also as the most glorious moment of all. Before then, I had not walked or spoken or eaten for hundreds of years. My existence was rather blunt and led me to feel as though I wasn't really alive at all. I was given a false reality, and yet, it was my reality nonetheless.

I was confined to the trees and the earth beneath them. I suppose it may have been a form of punishment for my unique set of abilities, or perhaps it was just a result of those who had a powerful knack for cruelty. During this plain reality, I watched the seasons fade each year as a restless prisoner until an innocent opportunity finally revealed itself to me.

On some random day, at some random hour, at some not-so-random spot, a young girl came passing through the woods. She was no taller than the developing aspens, yet no shorter than the saplings. She had a head of dark hair that desperately needed to be groomed. Her movements were quick and disorderly like those of a child throwing a tantrum. Her face was soft, but her eyes were not. No, instead, they were filled with impassioned tears of rage. I can attest that a child so young should not feel such hatred.

I watched this girl intently, unable to take my sight off of her. I had been alone for so long and now this curious little being appeared out of the blue. Perhaps it wasn't so random after all.

The girl stomped around, mumbling to herself in an irate manner. With my ears in every inch of the forest, I was able to pick up each word that spewed from her mouth.

"Well, if he wants us to go homeless then that's just fine. You're just a kid, Shiloh. You have no idea what real life is like, Shiloh," the girl said in a mocking tone. She walked around aimlessly, tracing the dirt with a stick. She made deformed drawings of various people that she would repeatedly erase and draw again. "Maybe he shouldn't make such bad business decisions. Yeah, I'm a kid, but I know a stupid decision when I see one!" the girl shouted. Her voice was delicate, even despite the bursts of yelling.

I observed this distressed child until the sunlight no longer reached the tops of the trees. She went on and on about her family and all the horrible issues they had caused. She described her mother to be abusive and spoiled by her father. The girl had a great hatred for the woman and became more enraged every time she spoke of her. However, she described her father much differently.

He was not as cruel nor heartless as the mother, but simply ignorant. She claimed he was a simple-minded man with poor work efforts. The girl knew that his laziness and drinking would be the downfall of his own business, and eventually, their family.

To hear of her miserable life was a burden on my own mind. I had wanted to rid her of these issues, but my physical form would not allow me to. The most I could do was give a listening ear, perhaps not a physical one, but a subconscious that remained in the trees.

Nearly every day, for many consecutive years, the girl passed through the forest and each time, she had more complaints. I learned virtually every detail about little Shiloh's life, good or bad. I learned that her family lived on the land just past the treeline that divided her home from mine. Their cottage of a house was quite unkempt and needed almost every repair one could think of. Her father's "failing business" was a small, cheap haunted house. I had never heard of such a thing in my life until then, and truly, the idea captivated me beyond words. Shiloh claimed that she adored the unique field of work, yet its decay took over their entire lives. The girl was intelligent in many respects, although she often lacked success in her schoolwork. It was something she spoke of frequently. In fact, school seemed to be one of the most prominent and stress-provoking topics to start each day. Shiloh had a difficult time making friends, and the few she did have didn't care to stick around very long. It seemed that I was just about the only one who actually took input of her piteous life.

I watched her transform into a perspective young woman. In many ways, she reminded me of myself when I was still in my human form. Our appearances were fairly similar, yet Shiloh always looked so sweet. Every feature concerning her person was more tender than my own. Furthermore, we were both resentful towards the insufferable nuisance that was humanity and all the alienation that came with it. Yet, in all the ways were similar, there was always something quite distinctly different. My heart did not beat the same as hers. My soul was destined to be much darker.

During this time, I began to feel that we were friends, or at the very least, connected in some way. However, there are times when I doubt this belief due to the irrevocable fact that the girl could not see me. Yes, she saw the trees and the dirt and the shrubs, but she could not truly visualize my persona. As I previously mentioned, I was confined to these things, my soul stretched throughout each morsel of life in those woods.

You cannot imagine how deeply I wished to be free of my imprisonment. As much as I enjoyed the company of this girl and hearing of her experiences, that would not suffice. I needed to escape the brown, ridged bars I had been trapped behind for centuries. I made daily attempts to lead Shiloh in the direction of my cage, but her drunken father would always call her back before she could reach it.

But then, the day came when Shiloh finally traveled far enough to find me. Her mind was particularly distressed that evening and her self-control was slipping away. She sauntered off the path and into the tall, lush grass. Her gentle steps came to a stop and her gaze paused on a gigantic, red maple tree. Its branches stretched far and wide, leaving the ground beneath it fully shaded from the sun's rays. The bark was smooth and gray, not an ugly gray like the sky on a bleak winter day, but a dark, stormcloud gray that flaunted each defined shade. Each leaf glimmered like a ruby, presenting the perfect shine. Everything about the tree was absolutely *mesmerizing*.

Shiloh stared at it as though she were completely entranced. But then, she noticed a strange green glow radiating from underneath the bark. It pulsed like a poisoned heartbeat. The girl got closer to the astonishing sight, ignorant to what it was exactly that stood in front of her. Then, the glow began to stretch towards her, calling to her. And in return, Shiloh reached her own hand towards it. She placed her fingers over the bark and began to pull at it vigorously. The more the bark was stripped away, the stronger the light grew. Shiloh's eyes got bigger and bigger with wonder as she tore away the pieces.

All of a sudden, the emerald light formed into the shape of a hand and wrapped its fingers tightly around Shiloh's wrist. The girl tried so desperately to pull away, but in an instant, her entire body went limp.

I could not tell you what happened moments after because everything went dark. My sight was taken from me and I no longer heard the sounds of every living organism in the forest.

~ 2 ~

TUCKER

If there is one thing I can say I truly regret, it was the decision to ever step foot on that property. People will do irrational things when they're desperate, and well, I suppose in this case I was the desperate one. I could use the excuse that I had no clue what was going on or that I was never interested in the complex rumors, but that would be a flat-out lie. I had heard the cryptic tales of fantasy and the horrific new stories, yet I chose to push those aside because my mind sought the complete truth. That was the only way I would be able to fully know.

I was 17 at the time. My family was ready to throw me out of the house the second I turned 18. We were extremely poor and constantly on the verge of getting evicted; the concept of poverty wasn't exactly new to our small town of Sleepy Hollow thanks to all our money going toward the abundance of tourism. My parents' thought process was that if I wasn't another person they had to pay for, then maybe they'd be better off and save some money. Truthfully, they hated each other just as much as they hated me, but of course, I had never made any sort of vow with either of them. Obviously, it was pretty harsh for a kid to hear, but it's not like I wanted to live with them anyway. In fact, I saw it as a chance to escape. My dad was always an asshole towards me for as long as I can remember, and my mom, well, she wasn't any better. The only day she had ever dropped me off at school was on my very first day of kindergarten. The next day and every day after I was forced to ride my bike, and if my bike was broken or unusable for whatever reason, I had to walk. And let's just say, Sleepy Hollow isn't exactly one of the warmest places. It didn't matter how bitter cold it could be or how tired I was, I had no other choice. Keep in mind that the school was a half-hour bike ride on a good day, so imagine walking on a bad day. I'm sure my sister, Tessa, had the same experience. She left after she had just taught me to read, and I hadn't spoken to her since. My parents would constantly fight with her over the slightest things and she eventually got sick of the never-ending verbal and physical abuse.

I remember her face pretty well; we looked a lot alike. We had the same dark, wavy hair, the same tanned, olive skin, the same plain brown eyes, and the same straight nose. Looking back at it, we were practically the same person, but maybe that's why my parents hated us both so much. They couldn't handle Tessa, so they had me, but I was just the male version. I cannot express how much I missed having her around. She parented me more than my mom and dad ever had or ever would.

Much like my sister at that age, I was in dire need of a stable job if I ever planned to survive. I wasn't looking for anything in the fast food industry or the casual cashier job. There was no joy in sitting behind a counter all day while ungrateful people barked orders at you. I knew my options were limited with what little experience I had, but I also knew that I wanted to do something of interest, something that wouldn't turn me into a depressed addict of sorts who hated their occupation and everything about life itself.

After searching around for a little while, I finally found a place that called to me. There were online posts for a popular outdoor haunted house called "Soul of the Wilderness" that was only about a half-hour bike ride from where I lived. Typically, a place like that wouldn't be my kind of scene, but for some reason, I found the idea of working there absolutely thrilling. But then again, this was the same place that was littered with stories of gruesome disappearances. I had never put much thought into any of it because people always warned me to stay away. They claimed that visiting that place was an automatic death sentence, and yet, no one had any concrete evidence.

When I went back to school the next day I immediately told my two closest friends, Asher Castillo and Charli Brookes, about the idea.

Asher was the guy I'd known since before I could read. You wouldn't believe how many people thought we were brothers. We had most of the same features, except he kept his hair a bit longer than mine and there was the very obvious fact that he was always a lot bigger than me. He used to shove me around all the time when we were kids, and well, he still did by the time we got to high school. He had always been the more athletic one. When we got to high school, it seemed like every chance he got he was in the gym. There were plenty of occasions when he tried to convince me to go with him, but I always said no. I just was never into all that stuff. Besides, it was kind of fun to feel like you always had your own personal bodyguard.

Asher and I met Charli in 8th grade. She was taller than both of us at the time and had a reputation for being rough around the edges. I remember how our English teacher forced Asher and I to be in a group with her because nobody else had room in their groups. She was pretty closed off at first, not wanting to talk or contribute to the group in any way, but eventually, she warmed up to us. I think she must have realized that we weren't the ones who made rumors about her in the halls, but we actually just felt rather intimidated. I mean, at 13 years old this girl was more masculine than both of us combined. I found her style rather unique for that age. She always had her chocolate-colored hair pulled back in a messy ponytail and wore what you'd imagine a grungy, teenage boy to wear. As we got older her style became slightly more feminine, but her personality, well, let's just say she never grew out of teasing Asher and I or treating us like her little brothers. Her eyes were hazel, but you would only notice that if you actually got close enough to have a conversation with her. I also remember how her ears were always decorated from top to bottom with piercings. She expressed herself freely, despite what the other girls would say about her not acting feminine enough. I loved that about her; it reminded me of my sister.

The very moment I finished telling them my plan to work at the haunted attraction, they looked at me as though I was utterly insane. It was the same reaction anyone would have given, so I don't really know why I expected anything else.

"I just don't get it. Why would you want to work where a bunch of people have literally died?" Asher said rather loudly as we exited the school.

I tried to shush him, peeking around to see if anyone else had heard. "Those are all just rumors. There's been no proven evidence that any of those deaths were linked to Soul of the Wilderness."

"Yeah, but you gotta admit, that Farrington family isn't normal," Charli chimed in, "Running a haunted house is one thing, but getting accused of numerous different murders is on a whole other level. Their names have been all over the news for years. Besides, *you* in a haunted house? Doesn't seem very fitting for someone who hates horror."

I couldn't help but sigh. They both had valid points, but I still couldn't break the overwhelming feeling of curiosity that ate at my brain.

As we traveled down the plain gray sidewalk to our bikes, I made the decision then and there.

"It doesn't really matter because I'm going there later today for an interview," I told my friends.

Charli rolled her eyes as she pulled her bike out of the rack. "Well, don't blame us if you get physically attacked while you're there," she mumbled.

"He won't even be able to do that 'cause he'll probably be dead," Asher said humorously.

I laughed along with them, ignoring the serious nature of it.

We rode our bikes down to the old church, just like every other day. The structure was dilapidated to the point where it seemed like it was ready to collapse at any moment, and yet, somehow, it still felt like a safe place to be. The building was hidden enough by the surrounding trees for us to be the only ones still using it. We would always climb in through one of the shattered windows since the doors were boarded shut. After years of using it, we felt as though it were a second home. It was a spot for us to shut out the rest of the world's issues and find peace, even if it only lasted for a little while. I found that quite important. I suppose it was one of the few things in life that truly kept me sane.

As the three of us sat in the old church, a body of gray clouds swept over the sky, engulfing every last bit of sunshine. The bright greens and yellows of the leaves faded only slightly, their pigment never faltering. They trembled in the slight breeze, only the most delicate falling from their place among the branches. The gust grew stronger and I watched calmly as the trees swayed in sync. The beauty of their movement was a miracle in itself.

Charli and Asher chattered quietly in the background. They bickered and scoffed in the way a brother and sister might. Charli fiddled with strands of her hair while Asher fought to explain whatever point he was trying to make this time. But then, like usual, I unwillingly got dragged into the conversation.

"Tucker, who made better pancakes yesterday? Me or him?" Charli asked with her arms folded.

I looked at them both with a muddled expression. They always fought over the most ridiculous things. It took me a second to even understand how or why they were talking about pancakes.

"How would he know? He left for half the class," Asher glared at her. "Besides, Ms. Hughes liked mine more than yours."

Charli's jaw dropped. "Oh, that's a load of garbage! Your pancakes literally tasted like dogshit," she argued aggressively.

"Yeah, you would know, huh?" Asher teased.

I turned my head back to the window as the two of them continued to fight. Their yelling eventually faded to simple background noise as I zoned out. All of a sudden, the wind became still. A chill tingled up my spine and the hairs on my arms stood straight up. A much darker overcast than just the clouds above took over the scene in front of me. My eyes locked onto the forest. It was almost as if the trunks of the trees began to bend and curve in such a way that formed a perfect gap right through the center. My heart stopped as a shadowy tunnel formed. It led to a single area of total darkness. Not a single outline or glimpse of light could be seen. I squinted, trying to see if there was anything in the darkness. For the briefest of moments, I saw the faint outline of a figure beginning to take shape. I could almost see it trying to reach a hand out, as if calling me to it.

Just then, my soul nearly left my body as a hand touched my shoulder. I spun around to see Charli and Asher staring at me in bewilderment.

"What's wrong with you?" Charli questioned, looking me up and down suspiciously.

For a second, I struggled to catch my breath. I realized that I must have been staring out that window for much longer than I could comprehend.

"N-nothing. I just thought I saw . . . nevermind. I'm just stressed about the interview."

"You should be," Charli cackled.

Asher smirked at her joke but soon changed his demeanor. "Hey, I'm sure you'll do fine. You've got charm and good manners. I'd be more surprised if they turned you down. Just," he sighed, "Please don't get yourself into anything stupid."

"Right," I nodded.

They both gave me reassuring smiles, although Charli's, per usual, was a little less sincere. She was trying to be nice, but she was never the best at hiding what she really thought. And usually, that came in the form of some facial expressions. I no longer took offense to it because at least she preferred to be honest.

We scrambled out of the old church and said our good-byes for the day before riding back to our houses.

To no surprise, a grubby, middle-aged man was passed out on the couch when I walked through the front door. That unfortunate soul was my father. The TV was playing some random news station, its light illuminating the dark room. I gently grabbed the empty beer bottle from my dad's hand and placed it in the kitchen. I crept down the hall, unable to avoid the creaky floorboards beneath my feet. I peeked into each open room, but it appeared that my mom wasn't home yet – thankfully.

When I finally reached my bedroom at the end of the hallway, I shoved the few things I needed for the interview into my backpack and headed right back out the door. I didn't like staying in that house too long. I never felt welcome.

~ 3 ~

TUCKER

I pedaled down the road in a hurry, my bike jolting with each split in the tar. The outdated chain around the tires squealed as I increased pace. I checked my phone frequently to make sure I wouldn't be late. I hated being late, yet it happened more than I'd like to say.

The closer I got, the more the air around me felt different, outlandish almost. In our tourist-ridden town, it was almost always rush hour, but today there were hardly any cars around. The sun divided the clouds perfectly to reveal its golden rays. As I glanced up, the moon was faintly visible from the bright blue background. Out of nowhere, I felt my spirit lift as a strike of energy flickered through my core. From that point on nothing felt real.

With little traffic I was able to make it to the haunted house in about half the time it should have taken me. Located on the hill, next door to the place, were a few small, crappy stores and a bar. Somehow, the bar was the most civilized-looking thing there.

I stopped my bike at the edge of a wide dirt road that split into two directions. Straight ahead was the dusty parking lot that was occupied with only a few vehicles. To the right of the split road was a tiny house, practically smaller than a cottage. It sat across from a giant red barn. The paint on both structures looked old and faded as it peeled off the sides. The more I looked around, the more it seemed like I was at a farm rather than an outdoor haunted house. The only part I found slightly eerie about the place was the considerable amount of noise that resonated from the woods in the back, which made sense at the time since that's where the actual haunted attraction was located.

I got back on my bike and rode towards the cottage. As I got farther down the dirt road, I discovered another structure that was hidden from sight behind the barn. It was about half the size and covered in opaque plastic sheets. The light created faint silhouettes of obscure shapes and movements from inside.

As I laid my bike on the ground, my ears tuned in to the voices from inside the greenhouse. I made my way over to it hesitantly as the nerves kicked in. I took a deep breath with each step, my rundown shoes kicking up dirt. As I listened to the voices, I realized that they were the only thing I could hear. Typically, a heavily wooded area like this would be thriving with the songs of birds or chirping of crickets, but there was nothing. Nothing at all.

Suddenly, the door to the structure swung open with a clang. I stopped dead in my tracks and waited for what was about to unfold.

A small group of grungy adults sauntered out. They seemed irritable by the way they shoved past me with resentment. They all had the same moody look, or maybe it was just their poorly done goth makeup. I assumed that they had also been there for interviews and all got denied. Besides the obvious style differences, they looked much like me – young and inexperienced, which struck a nerve of worry in the back of my head. I only saw them leaving for a split second before my eyes were inclined to watch the next occurrence.

At the entrance to the greenhouse stood a man who seemed about my father's age. He was short and over-weight with no sense of interview attire. I can't say my clothes were the image of prim and proper, but this guy looked like he had literally woken up in a horse stall five minutes beforehand.

I casually followed after him and waited by the doors as he entered.

He kept his hands clasped together behind his back as he wandered around the greenhouse, ignoring the other people but casually making his presence known. The man glanced around at the elaborate array of work supplies and Halloween decorations on the walls of shelves. He then tapped the shoulder of a younger man who was stocking a shelf with prop masks. The employee practically looked like a skeleton in comparison. Startled, he let one of the masks fall from his hands as he stared back, almost fear-fully, at the man.

"Can I speak to Ms. Farrington?" the burly man asked.

The employee pointed to the back of the greenhouse with a shaky finger.

At that exact moment, the most alluring human any of us had ever seen emerged through the small congregation of people. It was a young woman with a tall, slender, statuesque figure. Her sleek, pitch-black hair complimented the perfectly smooth, pale skin of her face. She had pronounced cheekbones and blood-red lips. The elegant choice of clothes she wore was almost as black as her hair. And her neck and hands were glamorized in the most peculiarly grim, yet intriguing jewelry. One piece that stood out in particular was a ring on the middle finger of her left hand. It was a golden snake that wrapped around her finger with emerald-colored eyes just like her own. Something about it caught my attention for an absurdly long time.

She approached the man slowly and dauntlessly, the heels of her shoes clicking against the floor. The man held out his hand in a similarly confident manner, but the woman just looked him up and down with intense judgment.

I crept a bit closer to listen in on their conversation, trying to get pointers on how not to screw up the interview.

"Are you Ms. Farrington?" the man asked, placing his arms behind his back once more.

"I am," the woman replied in a euphonic voice.

"It's a pleasure to meet you. I'm David Hall and uh, I'm here to interview for the job," he proudly smirked.

Ms. Farrington continued with her unrelenting gaze.

I couldn't quite see the smaller details of her eyes from where I was standing, but I knew for a fact that they were fierce.

A short moment of silence passed before she finally gave her response. "No," she stated plainly.

The man began to chuckle awkwardly. "What do you mean 'no'? You've barely spoken to me," he said.

"I *mean* you will not be working here," Ms. Farrington spoke coldly.

The man's chuckling turned into slight huffs of anger. He looked all around him with a furrowed brow. "I just got here," his hands flared out, "And you immediately turn me down? How is that fair? I don't understand."

"I am an extremely good judge of character, Mr. Hall, and one glance may be all I need. With you, it is clear to me that I could never have a mind like yours working for my business. I suggest you accept it and continue on promptly," the woman explained.

I was amazed and a little frightened at how eloquently she spoke. At some points, it even sounded like she had a bit of an accent.

Just as she started to walk away, the belligerent man grew even more outraged. "This ain't even your business, sweetheart! It belonged to your father and he did a much better job of runnin' it! You've turned it into some freak show!" the man shouted.

Everyone else in the greenhouse turned their attention to the scene. The expressions on their faces were both confused and horrified, yet none of them said a word.

Ms. Farrington turned back to the man coolly, her gaze

towering over his. "My father was a drunken fool who could barely stand on his own two feet, let alone run a business," she lowered her voice. "Now, I advise you leave my property before something regrettable happens, Mr. Hall. Anthony will ensure you get back to your vehicle without any ... *trouble.*"

The scrawny employee from earlier nervously made his way over to the man, ushering him to the exit. Ms. Farrington turned her back indifferently to the man who continued to yell indecent remarks, even when he got to the parking lot.

I watched him intently as he drove off the property in his red truck that was far too big for him. I thought by that point that I'd have no chance at even saying one word to Ms. Farrington and my heart sank. I turned around to get one last look at the strange greenhouse when I real-ized that the woman was standing directly behind me. I jumped back in alarm. All she gave me was a blank stare.

"I-I'm sorry. I didn't mean t-to-" I stuttered uncon-trollably.

"May I help you?" she said, still staring me down.

Usually, in such a nervous situation I would be avoid-ing eye contact by all means necessary, but this time I couldn't look away. This woman's eyes were incomparable to any other person's. They were like those of a snake – a sharp shade of green and intricately detailed all the way to the narrow pupil.

"Uh, uh, yeah. I mean, yes, sorry. Yes. I was hoping to get an interview for one of the open positions, of course, only i-if it's possible," I continued to stutter, fidgeting with my hands.

That's when I saw her gaze soften. Her perfectly red lips formed a gentle smile and she completely flipped her demeanor. "Of course, darling. I apologize for the prolonged wait. These people can be particularly bad-mannered," Ms. Farrington said calmly. She gestured for me to follow her into the greenhouse. "What's your name?" she questioned.

"Tucker Romero, ma'am," I replied, trying to keep up with her fast-paced steps. I didn't understand how she could move so swiftly in those heels.

She then stopped and spun around to face me. "You may call me Shiloh," the woman held out her hand.

I nodded and shook her hand dubiously, surprised by how well everything seemed to be going.

"You have a unique soul, Mr. Romero," Shiloh commented, reverting to that same peculiar stare.

As I mentioned previously, her eyes almost flawlessly matched those of a snake. And I swear to you that in that split second of a moment, her eyes dilated into slits. I blinked a few times to see if I was just imagining it and by the time I looked back, her eyes were normal again.

Shiloh continued to guide me through the greenhouse until she came across the employee who she had summoned earlier. "This is Anthony. He has been one of my most loyal members for over three years," she stated.

The man stared at me with wide, sunken eyes. His reddish hair was thinning and his beard was unkempt. For a grown man, he appeared to be severely underweight. His raggedy clothes stunk of cigarette smoke, which also was a possible explanation as to why he looked so unhealthy. Everything about him was depressing.

Something even more odd about him that I noticed was the small slip of paper in his clenched fist. Sketched on the paper was a grim face with horns. The face almost looked like a child's drawing of the Devil.

I didn't put too much thought into the drawing and held out my hand, but he refused to take it. Instead, he began to shake his head more and more rapidly. That's when Shiloh snapped her fingers right in front of his face.

"Anthony, would you please go to the barn and change out the drill batteries?" she announced in a gentle yet assertive manner.

The man nodded repeatedly and hurried out the door.

"I hope you will forgive him. He's been quite ill lately," Shiloh said with a dismal expression.

"Oh. I-I'm sorry. What is it that's making him sick?" I asked.

"Well, you see, it's not an ailment of the body, but rather an ailment of the mind. He claims to see horrible fantasies during the night, fantasies that seem so life-like," she explained.

"That sounds awful," I said piteously.

"Yes, it is. So, I must warn you, Tucker," she brought her voice down to a whisper, "An unusual place such as a haunted house may do strange things to our minds. That is why only certain people are capable of fully executing the job. Do you think you will be able to handle the bizarre nature of it all?"

Her words sent such a shiver down my spine that I debated leaving right then and never coming back. It was obvious that Ms. Farrington embraced the spooky lifestyle of owning a haunted house, but I considered that a good thing. It meant she was passionate about her work. Boy, was I right about that.

"I can handle whatever God needs me to do," I told her confidently.

She smirked ever so slightly. "Welcome to Soul of the Wilderness, Mr. Romero," Shiloh stated firmly.

I grinned wider than I had ever grinned before. There were no words to express how relieved I felt knowing that I had found a job. "Thank you! Thank you so much," I said excitedly.

"I'll see you back here tomorrow for orientation. Four o'clock," she asserted.

"Absolutely," I responded, still with that naive grin on my face.

I rushed outside and picked up my bike, the buzz of elation running thick through my veins. But that happiness soon died out when something else caught my attention. The forest at the back of the property was still buzzing with noise like it was when I had first arrived, but now, the trees appeared to me with a mesmerizing existence.

Just then, I made the worst decision possible for that moment. It was the decision that sparked my curiosity and pushed it to its absolute limit. I got onto my bike once more and traveled towards the clearing in trees.

The closer I got, the more my heart pounded. I blocked out any noise that came from my bike and focused solely on that which echoed from the forest. A pit formed in the center of my stomach, warning me not to go any further, but I stupidly ignored it. I got off the bike and all of a sudden, the tension disappeared into thin air as the most enchanted-looking rays of pure, golden light cut through the trees. There wasn't a single breeze or stirring movement from beyond. The trunks of the trees appeared to grow immensely tall, their bark stretching miles high. I could've sworn they were calling out to me, speaking in hushed whispers, trying to drag me farther in. My mind ran blank and I allowed the beauty of the woods to guide me. I took one step, then another, and another. On the sixth step, my foot crossed over the dividing line and I entered the perimeter of the forest. The glow was becoming blinding.

Just before I could fully cross over, a voice sounded from behind me.

"I'm afraid we'll have to save that venture for another day," Shiloh called out.

I hadn't realized she had followed me, and I clumsily tripped back into the open. "Sorry, sorry. I just wanted to see what it actually looked like in there," I mumbled, frantically trying to defend myself.

"Oh, you're quite alright. It's enchanting, I'm aware. I just don't want you to spoil your own fun before I introduce you to the others, that's all," she said reassuringly.

Not knowing what else to do, I gave an exaggerated nod.

"Tomorrow," she said before walking casually back towards the cottage.

I kept my head down as I picked up my bike. I was so

shaken that my hands struggled to find the handles and my feet the pedals.

After that, I raced home out of pure humiliation.

~ 4 ~

METSAH

When I awoke, Shiloh's body was on the ground, as was mine; we had become one. I had regained all the physical senses and functions that make a person human, except none of it truly belonged to me. I was beyond thrilled to have limbs and fingertips and toes once more. Of course, in the back of my mind, sat the overarching fear of only remaining in that state temporarily. I couldn't bear to let it go, to let my soul be separated from this living body, to let life itself be taken from me once again. So, I ensured that my death may only be guaranteed by the raging scorch of my entirety, not just skin and bones, but the natural surface that my soul was still madly connected to.

The light in the sky had departed and the eyes of angels glared down at me from above. As I rose up, the earth beneath my feet had never felt sweeter. Sparks of energy overflowed the grains of soil with every divided step I took. My lungs propelled breath through the trees as wind through my hair. The darkness of night clung to me, unable to let go. I had never felt a stronger connection to the natural world in all of my being.

The farther I traveled, the warier I became about leaving my home. I stood at the edge of the trees and let my eyes wander. They were struck with reminiscence of the relative ugliness of the world from prior involvement, yet now everything seemed to be set aflame with filth. With the time humanity had been given, one would think they would make improvements to their lifestyles and value the natural gifts around them. But they did not. Humanity caused their own abhorrent demise. This outside territory was an abomination and even setting foot on it ignited an incomparable disgust within me. I hated the world, truly, wholly, uncontrollably.

When I attempted to retreat to my home, I was miserably reminded of interruptions that would soon inevitably appear to me. Governing as Shiloh brought along the unfortunate circumstances that were her family, and to my dismay, they had to be dealt with. Therefore, if it had to be done, I preferred to make this opportunity as desirable as possible for myself.

I wandered back to the red leaves of my origin in search of a proper solution. I envisioned my desire with the utmost willpower until the hand of the Dark One sprouted from the ground and there appeared my answer. A flower, so delicate in nature, stood at my feet. From the root of its stem to the tip of its innocently pink petals, a deadly fate lay disguised. I accepted the gift, my soul once more in debt. With this favor resting in my hand, I found myself entirely compelled to search for the structure in which Shiloh slept.

The utmost dread surged through me as I crossed the barrier into the world, yet something quite unexpected occurred. Ascendancy flowed over both the body and mind. As I peered around, I realized there was no need to fear. No being such as Shiloh could surmount the power that had been given to me and now resonated in my presence. I was the one to be feared, not them.

I strolled the path until I came to a humble structure. A warm glow illuminated the windows, welcoming me to enter. As I set foot in the entryway, a groggy male voice sounded from somewhere within the house.

"Shiloh, is that you?" The words echoed softly off the walls. "Are you alright, darling? Come here," the voice called.

I assumed my due diligence as this girl and approached the room from which I heard the man. Upon seeing him for the very first time, I promptly concluded that this must be her father – my father. All that she had said was exact. The man that appeared before me flawlessly fit the description in every way; he lay on the couch like a slovenly disgrace with no cognizance of his own wretchedness.

I neared my father in great hesitance.

When his drooping eyes finally noticed my shadow standing only a foot away, his expression was shrouded with a pleasant smile. "Shiloh," he mumbled, "You missed dinner again. Your mom wasn't happy, but what's new? Oh, look at you, you have a pretty flower."

I couldn't bring myself to speak. I could only study

this being with curiosity. Had so much time gone by? I had seen pathetic, drunken men previously, and men who were unable to confront their sufferings, but was this truly to be the common way of living?

My father peered down at the rug I stood on, his smile ever fading. "Why didn't you put shoes on while you were out there? It-it's chilly, kid . . ." he veered off.

I glanced down at my own feet. At the time, I couldn't think of any reason why one would place coverings over their feet unless the ground had been layered in jagged stones or contaminated with poison oak. Seeing that the only current threat appeared to be dirt, I ignored the man's cretinous comments.

When I faced him once more, my father was dormant. His eyelids rested peacefully over one another and with each heave of his chest, a deep grumble was released. I remained observant over him momentarily, but boredom quickly overtook me.

As I continued to explore the rest of this house, I was suddenly reminded of my purpose for being there in the first place. An obscure flash of light shone through the windows. In the following moments, a disturbance of loud noises arose from the entrance of the house. I stood in the hallway, patiently awaiting the arrival of yet another being. I must inform you that my mood was instantly brought up when I discovered who it was. The woman that Shiloh had said forced so much misery into her life, the woman who despised her family, the woman who was so far gone . . . that woman walked in. Indeed, she did not match the sweet persona of Shiloh or even the unfortunate nature of her own husband. This woman was the ideal image of humanity in all its disgrace and sin. She stopped dead in her tracks when she noticed me. I was ecstatic, to say the least, when this woman scowled at her daughter's face because it so clearly verified every previous reason I had to detest her.

I can say for certain that I had no remorse about killing Shiloh's mother – my mother. It was a rather thrilling experience, as simple as it was. I slept not a wink that night, preparing the flower so discreetly. The touch alone of one of its petals could infect a human's bloodstream with dire toxicity, so you can only imagine the effects it would leave when I snuck the entire lifeform into the woman's breakfast.

I watched her closely that morning, despite the pure aversion I felt from being nearby. She was so clueless, so ignorant, so blatantly futile. Seeing her sip her morning coffee so casually was almost laughable. By the time she finished eating, there was hardly any time left for her, and only *I* knew. She stood up from the table with the plate in hand and her body became stiff. I feel deeply in my heart that she must've known it was I who betrayed her. A look of realization crept into her eyes when she saw me there, silently watching with a most satisfied smile. Her breathing began to slow and the base of her skin grew hideously pale. It was over so quickly that I had nearly wished that I could have prolonged her suffering.

Wisely, I disappeared from the scene until my father called me in to inform me. That drunken fool never had a clue what actually happened. Along with everyone else, he was blinded by the overwhelming facade of virtue and beauty that I had created for Shiloh, and I intended to keep it that way.

~ 5 ~

TUCKER

For once in my life, I couldn't wait for the weekend to be over. I was desperate to go back to school and tell Asher and Charli all about the new job. I knew they would probably say I was crazy again, but I expected nothing less.

The second I walked through the door to my history class, Asher was already looking at me. He waved me over in a hurry, his eyes wide with anticipation.

"So, how'd it go?" he asked as I slid my backpack under my desk.

"Oh my gosh, dude. It was so horrible," I said.

He furrowed his brow. "Really?"

I paused for a moment, allowing the shock to sink in. Then, I glanced at him with a smirk. "Just kidding," I laughed, "I got the job."

Asher nearly shoved me right out of my desk. "You're a moron," he muttered, trying to hide his smile. "You know, Charli's probably gonna try to get you to quit, right?" he added.

"Oh I'm sure," I told him, staring at the front of the room.

He looked at me blankly. "So . . . that's it? Nothing interesting happened while you were there? Like, did you see anything strange? Are any of the rumors true?"

I thought back to the whole experience. There were obvious moments that stuck out in my mind, like the odd behavior from the owner herself or the enchanting hold that the forest had on me, but I chose to leave that out. I didn't want Asher to take Charli's side before he even got a chance to see it for himself.

"Well, for a haunted house, it seems pretty tame. The other people looking for jobs are probably the worst part. Let's just say, Ms. Farrington doesn't put up with anyone's shit," I told him.

"How many people work there besides you?"

"That's actually a good question, but I don't have an answer. I only met one guy and it doesn't seem like he's all there," I said. I pictured Anthony's strange behavior; there was a sort of derangement in his eyes that I could never forget. "Ms. Farrington probably just gave him a job out of pity. She said I would meet the others another day, which might mean today or maybe even later," I explained.

Asher nodded, taking very little time to move on from the conversation. He relocated his focus to the papers that were getting handed out to the class.

I couldn't help but bring up the subject once more; my nerves were still on edge. "You should try for a job there too," I whispered to Asher as the teacher began the lecture.

He turned to me with a perplexed expression. "Why would I do that? I still don't trust that place."

I shrugged, stumbling to find a convincing argument. "Well, you need a job, don't you?"

"Yeah, but I'd rather not die on the clock," Asher said gruffly, turning his head back to the front.

"You won't," I nudged his arm.

He side-eyed my hand.

"At least just go and see it for yourself. You can come with me on Friday during opening night, that way Ms. Farrington has time to warm up to me a little more and she's more likely to say yes. Just please attempt it, Asher," I looked at him sincerely.

"Fine. But only because I need to find a job," he mumbled, trying to pretend he was listening to the lecture.

A satisfied grin grew across my face. I believed that if Shiloh Farrington had taken such a strong liking to me, there was no way she wouldn't like Asher as well.

The rest of the day took forever to get through. Each time I glanced at the clock, the hour and minute hands seemed to slow. They would tease me with their gradual ticks, the noise becoming deafening. For the most part, I was beyond excited to go to the orientation and finally start working, but a small piece of me was filled with this taunting anxiety that just wouldn't go away. I shoved that feeling as far back in my brain as I possibly could, leaving no room for doubt.

As soon as the bell rang out through the school, I raced outside to my bike, my hasty footsteps echoing down the halls. All kinds of strange looks were thrown in my direction as I brushed past other kids on the sidewalk, my backpack bouncing with each step.

I was pulling my bike from the rack when I heard a familiar voice call my name.

"Tucker!" a girl shouted.

I glanced up to see Charli staring me down with her arms crossed from one of the school doors. Her hair was tied up in her usual messy ponytail and it appeared that she was still wearing her gym clothes. She waved at me with a furrowed brow. "Tucker! Where are you going in such a rush?" she called.

"I-I-"

Her expression only became more confused as I stood there gawking without giving a clear response. I knew she'd try to stop me if I told her right then that I had gotten the job, but then again, I didn't want to lie to her.

"Work!" I finally said, frantically pointing in some random direction behind me. I quickly hopped on my bike and pedaled in the opposite direction, leaving Charli alone by the door with no explanation. Once I got to the open road, I briefly looked back. She had disappeared back inside the building. I let out a sigh of relief, but when I turned my head forward again, my bike came to a sudden halt. The sound of screeching tires roared in front of me. I placed one foot on the ground, my heart pounding.

"Watch where you're going! You shouldn't even have a bike on this road!" a red-faced man shouted from the open window of his car.

"S-sorry. Sorry. I didn't see you," I rambled stupidly. I truly don't think I could have looked like more of an idiot than I did at that moment. I almost got myself run over from my own pure negligence.

The irate man kept a scowl on his face and sped off in his car, mumbling foul obscenities that were obviously directed at me.

I tried my best to shake off the sudden nerves that had just overcome me and continue to the haunted house. During the rest of my journey there, I experienced, what I thought at the time, was the worst luck ever. But now, I look back at it and realize that God had only been trying to save me. About halfway there, one of my tires went flat from the piercing of a jagged nail, yet there was no reason for a nail to be that far away from any form of housing or construction. Then, as I was trying to make up for the slowed pace, I discovered that cops had closed down the road I was on due to a severe car accident. I argued with them over why they wouldn't let a bike pass by, but they threatened to put me in cuffs if I didn't turn around. I ended up finding a way into the surrounding woods after the cops were distracted enough by the actual serious situation at hand that was the car accident. Of course, this only delayed me more, but by then I was able to reach the haunted house with no other troubles.

When I arrived in the dirt parking lot, I immediately checked the time on my phone. Frustration struck me when I realized it was already ten minutes past four. I threw my bike down and ran to the greenhouse, kicking up dust as I went. I tried to look through the some-what see-through walls of the structure, but there was no movement.

All of a sudden, I heard an intense breathing from behind me. I spun around and saw Anthony, the one employee I met. He was just staring at me, his bloodshot eyes straining to focus on my own. His already scraggly beard seemed thinner than before like he had ripped the hair right from it.

"Do you know where Shiloh is?" I asked him, shifting uncomfortably in my stance.

Anthony continued with his deranged stare. As I tried to step past him, he began shaking his head back and forth as he did the day before. I stopped and waved my hand in front of his face to try and get him out of this trance-like state.

"Anthony, are you okay?" I questioned.

Suddenly, he froze. He opened his mouth slightly as if to say something, but it seemed that some sort of fear was holding him back.

"Anthony," I repeated.

Without ever blinking, he uttered, "No. No. There is no escape."

I stared back at him in confusion. "What?"

"No, there's never a chance. The eyes are everywhere," Anthony continued to ramble on, tilting his head down at the ground. His face was frightened once more and his eyes were filled with wild tears. He placed his hands on the side of his head and began ripping at his hair furiously.

I placed my hands on his shoulders, attempting to calm him. "Anthony, what are you talking about?" I said. I tried to hold him still but he moved around frantically in circles, eventually blocking my path to the greenhouse.

Just then, his head shot back up and his eyes peered through my soul. There was no way of describing the absolute insanity in this man's expression.

"We're trapped! Their eyes are everywhere!" he screamed, the veins in his neck straining all at once.

I recoiled back, surprised by his sudden outburst. The man continued to block my path until a figure in all black appeared behind him.

"Anthony," her red lips spoke serenely.

The man became motionless at the sound of her voice. He stared back at me, the fear in his eyes rising.

"Turn around," Shiloh said with her hands clasped together.

Anthony slowly began to face her, his limbs stiff as wood. I dropped my hands from his shoulders cautiously.

"Go back to work, Anthony," the woman said, narrowing her eyes at him. "Now," her voice became harsher.

Anthony gradually wandered away, taking careful steps. His movements were strained, even when he was a great distance away from us. My eyes followed him until he was no longer in my line of vision.

"Once again, my apologies, Mr. Romero. I try to keep him under control, but it seems his . . . *condition* is only getting worse," she told me. Her voice was so mesmerizing.

"I-I'm sorry to hear that."

"Yes, as am I. I'm afraid Anthony may not be with us much longer if he continues his ways," Shiloh said, beginning to walk toward the barn.

I moved alongside her, hesitant to walk too slow or too

fast. "What do you mean? Are you going to fire him?" I questioned, looking up at her occasionally.

"Not by choice. I simply mean that he is in a rather melancholic state. And, well, melancholy often messes with our heads. It drags us to our lowest points and all of a sudden we believe it may just be easier to take our own lives, rather than deal with the things we don't like. I fear Anthony is getting closer to that stage at a rapid rate," she explained as we walked.

I peered up at the sky, expecting to see gray, but instead, I saw a blanket of blue. It was nature at its finest.

Shiloh slid open the barn doors and welcomed me inside. I was astounded, to say the least, at what I saw when the light poured in. My mouth opened in awe. Encapsulating the entire floor were custom-made Halloween props that were yet to be finished. There were rows of monsters and ghouls and fiends that I had never even imagined could exist. They had the strangest faces, the ugliest hands, and the most terrifying smiles. I quickly took notice of the one thing they all had in common: none of them had eyes.

"Don't you love them?" Shiloh voiced, flicking on a light switch.

I began to walk through the lengthy rows of monsters. "This is incredible. They all look so life-like," I said, fascinated by the creations. "How did you even come up with all of these? I mean, this must've taken ages to do," I muttered, glancing back at her.

A pleased grin ran across Shiloh's face as she waited patiently by the doors. "It took years of practice. I knew that I needed to perfect each one before letting the world see them," she said.

The woman sauntered through the rows just as I had, her eyes transfixed on the different beasts. I swear it was like they were all looking back at her, even with their lack of eyes.

Just then, Shiloh turned to look at me. "Tucker, I need you to understand what they mean to me. They have been with me from start to finish. I added every single minuscule detail on them that you are seeing at this very moment. They are my creations ... my *children*."

I blinked awkwardly, not knowing if I was supposed to give a response.

"In the past, others have treated them as nothing more than garbage – objects that they can toss around and destroy as they like. But I don't think you are one of those people. I believe you will treat my creations and every-thing else in this attraction with respect, will you not?" she spoke.

"Of course. I wouldn't want to do anything to offend you or the work you've put into this place. I think it's all amazing. I can't believe people would even do things like that," I babbled, my fast-paced words blending together.

"Good. Then we can move on to the other areas of the property," Shiloh told me, heading to the doors.

I followed her out of the barn, and as she slid the doors shut, I saw the face of every single one of those creatures look back at me as if to say goodbye.

~ 6 ~

TUCKER

After visiting the barn, we went directly to the greenhouse. Shiloh warned me not to touch anything before entering. She seemed quite serious about whatever she was working on inside. I did as she said, not wanting to lose my job before it even began.

The inside of the greenhouse was almost exactly the same as the way I saw it last. The disturbing masks lined the shelves and Halloween decor hung everywhere. Each object was in its usual place, except for one item; in the farthest corner was the structure of a human, built from PVC pipes.

"Shiloh, what's that?" I asked curiously, pointing to the odd construction.

"Ah, that's one of my newest friends I've been working on," she responded, walking alongside the structure. "You see, I must start with the pipes as a base layer for all of them. Think of it as their skeleton. Then, over time, I add the materials I need in order for them to appear as real as possible." She folded her arms with a slight grin. "This allows me to truly bring them to life."

"Well, you've done a good job at that. The other ones seemed pretty life-like to me," I chuckled.

The woman's eyes focused on the formation of pipes intently. I could see her imagining her final creation right then and there.

"When do you think you'll finish that one?" I asked in a hesitant tone, wary of being too intrusive.

"I'm not quite sure. That will depend on other circumstances – those of which have not yet occurred." Shiloh never took her eyes off the structure as she spoke. She never even blinked.

I continued to glance around the greenhouse, waiting for her to move on to the next thing. I didn't want to let her see that I was anxious, so I stopped myself from fidgeting or swaying. Instead, I was probably more awkward with how unnaturally still I became.

After a short moment, she turned her attention back to me. "So sorry, Tucker. I have an unfortunate habit of getting lost in my thoughts. It's a bit more extreme than I care to say," she said.

I gave her that dumb smile I always got when I felt awkward. That expression was practically permanent on my face.

"Now, let us continue," she announced, gesturing to the exit.

Shiloh then began to guide me through the rest of the property, explaining just enough to ensure that I wouldn't screw anything up. I'll admit that it was all pretty boring until we reached the entrance to the forest. Only a few feet in front of us stood a twisted, wooden arch with moss laced all around it. There were fragile twigs and leaves attached sporadically, yet perfectly. The words "Soul of the Wilderness" were etched deeply into the wood. It looked like something out of a fairytale. But then, I noticed the two grotesque, winged gargoyles that sat perched on top of the arch. Their faces were detailed with an identical, grim expression that seemed to threaten anyone who dared to enter. They had cuspate claws that dug into the wood to keep them balanced, and similarly sharp teeth. I know I shouldn't have been shocked when I saw that they were also missing eyes, but I was. I assumed that all of her finished creatures would have had them.

Shiloh made her way under the arch, motioning for me to follow. Looking at the entrance, I wasn't sure if I was filled with fear or excitement, but whatever it was, it definitely made my heart race.

I briefly looked up at the gargoyles overhead. They frightened me, they always frightened me. There was something about the way gargoyles all sat hunched over, looming above our heads and staring down at us like they could strike at any second. I didn't like that they were constantly watching, and it seemed like they knew that, in fact, it seemed like they took pleasure in it.

"What inspired you to make these?" I voiced as I scurried under the arch, keeping my eyes on the statues the entire time. Just as they would not break their gaze from me, I found myself unable to look away from them as well, leaving me unaware of what else was in that forest.

"They turned out beautifully. Don't you agree?" Shiloh said, admiring the grim statues.

"Well, yes, but why did you choose gargoyles? Aren't they meant to protect a place from evil or something like that?" I restated, examining the sculpted wings.

"A misleading statement. People made up myths such as this in an attempt to convince themselves that evil may be combatted when faced with something just as hideous . . . but it cannot be. That's just evil against evil, which is impossible considering they do not defy one another. 'Gargoyles' is just a fancy term. Those are demons you're looking at," Shiloh explained.

I finally tore my eyes away from the sculptures and looked at her. "So, you're *welcoming* evil?" I questioned.

The woman paused and glanced at me. At first, I thought that she had taken offense to the question and I had basically just thrown my job out the window.

But after a moment of thinking, she gave her answer. "People often misjudge demons. We think because they are hideous that they are purely meant to harm you. But the truth is, they can *help* you just as equally," she stated. Her eyes seemed to fluctuate between human and snake once again. "Now, come along. There is much more for you to see," Shiloh said, moving swiftly along the dirt trail.

As I followed after her, that same euphoric feeling returned to me from the first time I neared the woods. The sun was capturing all the beauty of the trees and the air that flowed between them. At the time, it didn't feel like I was standing on the ground of a haunted attraction at all, but instead, I was actually in the fairytale I had imagined only moments before.

"People are supposed to be afraid of this?" I mumbled mindlessly. That one offended her.

Shiloh shot a sudden glare in my direction. "I can assure you it's quite different in the night," she spoke sharply. The expression on her face seemed slightly irritated. "You'll find out soon enough, and then you can reconsider your words."

I knew I had made a mistake. But I didn't know that the last phrase she uttered would come back to haunt me.

We walked so slowly down the path that sometimes I questioned if we were even still moving until Shiloh completely stopped. Her eyes wandered all around, and then, a confused look appeared on her face. I was surprised because I had never seen her like that before; she had always seemed so certain of everything.

"W-what's wrong?" I asked hesitantly.

She immediately put her finger to her lips to shush me.

I froze in place, glancing around uncomfortably and wondering if she saw something I didn't.

"Do you hear anything?" Shiloh whispered softly.

"Um, no. No, I don't," I shook my head, re-examining all of my surroundings.

That slight grin returned to her face. "That's because they're hiding. They sense you, but they are not afraid of you nor angry with you," she said, staring at me.

Now, I was the one with the confused look on my face.

"I suppose my predictions were right. He does have a peculiar soul," the woman spoke as if she were talking to someone else. Her gaze softened. "Would you like me to show you?" she asked.

I furrowed my brow. "What do you mean? Show me what?"

Shiloh stepped beside a nearby tree and placed her hand gently on the bark. I watched nervously, afraid that I might get an axe in the neck or a bullet to the forehead at some point. The next few moments almost sent me into a state of shock. Shiloh closed her eyes and kept her hand on the tree. All of a sudden, an emerald-green glow appeared in the veins of her hand. The color transferred to the bark, lighting up each little crevice of the trunk. And then, all the trees in the woods began to shift, creating a rumbling in the ground. Their leaves began to shake as a powerful gust of wind began to pick up. I tilted my head towards the sky and stared up at the phenomenon with wide eyes. The increasing strength of the breeze started to push me off balance and my hair became disheveled.

"What's happening?" I asked, trying to make my voice louder than the wind.

Shiloh gave no response. Her eyes were still closed like she was peacefully asleep.

"H-how are you doing that?"

Just then, it all stopped. The air was calm once again. I finally looked away from the sky and saw Shiloh standing quietly next to the tree with her hands clasped together.

"What was that?" I questioned. I was more fearful of her after that than the first time I had ever seen her.

"I tried to summon them out of hiding but they refused.

They are afraid you will run off if they reveal themselves too early," she said.

A chill ran up my spine. I took her words to heart and now felt eyes on me from every angle. "Who is '*they*?'" I asked.

"The others. They will be working alongside you," she said bluntly.

I remained frozen.

The woman let out a hushed sigh. "I can see you're frightened. You do not need to be. Trust me when I tell you this, Tucker. They are not perilous . . . just . . . unique."

"So, let me get this straight," I held out my hands, "I'll be working with these people that I've never met before and they don't want me to see them? And you're acting like they're dangerous or something? Are they like mentally unstable? 'Cause I mean, Anthony doesn't seem too-"

"They are quite controlled, I promise. I am the very thing that keeps them stable," Shiloh interrupted.

I paused with a concerned look. "So are they going to be in costumes? Like the props you made?"

Shiloh gave a single nod. "Everyone else will fear them, but not you."

I sighed and ran my hands through my hair anxiously.

"Tucker, you can trust me. And as long as you can trust me, you can trust them. Your job will be to simply act as a security guard and help me make sure everything is running smoothly each night. You'll work on props, lighting, decorations, everything there is to do behind the scenes. Plus, the pay is $200 for each of the nine nights and extra compensation for the other days you want to come in to help," she explained.

I could hardly believe what she had just said. For where I lived, that amount would be making headlines.

"And what about after Halloween season, you know, when it's all over? Will you keep me employed?"

"Of course. I'll need to prepare for next year. It's a process that takes work every single day. That's why my haunt is so successful," Shiloh stated firmly. Her gaze softened once more, and I was reminded of my sister. "I know what your life is like at home, Tucker. I see the desire in your eyes to be rid of them and to finally be at peace. Here," she looked all around, "You can have that peace. You will be taken care of."

No, I didn't know how she knew. But she did. And my heart was begging me to trust her. The way she spoke of the haunt made everything feel completely normal, but that feeling in the back of my brain was screaming the exact opposite. I thought for a second, reminding myself that I had applied for a job at a haunted house and nothing about it was supposed to be normal. You might think I was stupid, and to be honest, I was. After everything she had just shown me, I don't know why I didn't just run right out of there.

"Okay," I huffed, "I guess I'll do it."

"Perfect." The woman began to casually walk back in the direction we came from as if none of that conversation had just happened. "You'll be back here on Friday, in the greenhouse. Arrive precisely by 4 o'clock. We do not appreciate tardiness here, Mr. Romero. Today was your one exception," she muttered, the pace in her steps quickening.

I followed behind, frantically trying to keep up with both the walking and her words. Before we got back to the entrance, I looked around one last time. Everything in the woods seemed to have gone back to normal as if the trees weren't just following Shiloh's magic command a few minutes ago and I had only imagined it. I felt like I was starting to "just imagine" quite a lot. But then, I noticed a piece of paper that had been caught in some nearby weeds. At first, it appeared to be blank until a soft breeze flipped it over. From what I could see, there was a drawing of a strange creature. It was pitch black and had the body of a human, but it was as if all its limbs had been oddly contorted. With one last glance, I could just make out what seemed to be wings on the creature. I assumed the drawing was just a sketch that Shiloh had made for one of her props or costumes.

Shiloh led me under the arch once more. I peeked back, hoping to catch those demons actually staring at me with real eyes and disturbed grins, but all I saw were two stone gargoyles, lifelessly sitting on the wood like the inanimate objects they were made to be.

When we returned to the greenhouse, I noticed a person standing at the top of the hill by the bar. The place was typically fairly vacant, at least during the day, so I was surprised to see another human being. As I squinted my eyes I could see that it was a man with a bitter expression on his face. At first, I thought he was looking at me, but then I realized he was staring down Shiloh. I glanced at Shiloh, wondering if she even noticed the man. Sure enough, she was already looking back at him. The two seemed to have some sort of previously formed tension that was irremissible.

"Uh, Shiloh? Who is that?" I spoke up.

The woman didn't even budge. Her sulky glare would not break from the man's gaze.

"Shiloh?" I repeated.

Finally, the man turned away and trudged back towards the bar. This broke Shiloh's undaunted stare and she began walking once more. I followed, waiting patiently for her to say something, anything.

Inside the greenhouse, she slammed the doors shut behind us. I flinched from the sudden disturbance. I stood with my arms at my sides and my eyes aimed at the ground, fearful that if I made one wrong move, Shiloh would really become violent.

"That *man*," Shiloh mumbled angrily under her breath. She started to fumble around with various items in the greenhouse with no sensical reasoning. "He'll be in a grave before I ever let him onto my land," she continued quietly.

I finally got the courage to speak again. "Shiloh, who is he?" I asked gently.

The woman stopped all her movements and straightened her stance. She turned around eerily slow and looked at me. "A liar," she hissed. Her eyes flashed with animosity. "That man has been trying to get me out of business ever since I took over for my father. He is an ignorant fool with not a clue of what he speaks."

I stared, terrified.

"Tucker, I'm sure you will hear awful things about me and this place – if you have not already. But my hope for you is that you can see for yourself that the things they have said are lies. We work in a place where fear is praised and loved, yet when people leave, they take that fear with them. And sadly, it twists their perception of truth. That man you saw is just one example. So please, Tucker, do not let anyone else's thoughts alter your own. I need to be able to trust you, and vice versa," the woman said.

I acknowledged her with a simple nod.

She gave a pleased half-smile. "Friday," she said.

I nodded again, this time more vigorously, and hurried out of the greenhouse to my bike.

~ 7 ~

METSAH

Ridding the Earth of Shiloh's mother, if you could call her that, was the first step to renewing myself. After the limited contact I had with the wretched woman, I knew she was no example of a mother at all. She despised her child more than life itself and so openly expressed it too. I knew that I could never allow myself to show even the slightest resemblance to her, ever. A mother is meant to have an undying love for her children, a love so far from breakable that not even her own life matters when they are in need. As an order from the one I feared most, I immersed my life with the care of my own creations, my own children. I was given their souls so that everything I did would be for their avail. I gave them each their first breath and I was the only one who could take it from them.

My father's specific type of business gave me the most ideal opportunity in which I could carry out this course of action. I busied myself with hours of ceaseless effort to master my work. My father grew worried at times, claiming a young girl shouldn't be doing such a thing, rather, he suggested I go out into the open world and connect with the other people my age. I dismissed him every time, having no interest in what he said. There was nothing I could say except that I preferred to surround myself with such a temporary loneliness because someday it would bring about an unmatchable success that no human being could attest to. My father's deep ignorance blinded him from the truth of my words and he allowed his young Shiloh to carry on.

After nearly a year of construction and revision, I held the very first tangible form that I could bring to life. I stepped back, gazing upon its magnificent face. It stood at the height of a small child and its latex skin was more real than any human flesh, although distinctly pale. Its ears were almost as large as its head and it had a strong, sharp jaw. And there was also the smile. Through the rows of jagged teeth was a devious little smile that always brought delight to my heart. The only piece missing was the very thing that gave it a soul: the eyes. The sockets would remain blank until I put my power to use.

In that moment, my father earned the only recognition I could ever have given him. He entered the room and observed the creature alongside me. He placed a hand on his chin and tilted his head. "Now that's one hell of a goblin," he snickered.

I glanced at him and then back at the creation. "A goblin," I repeated.

Although his contribution was slight, it still held a sense of importance in my work. He named my child for me that day and would continue to name nearly all of them. I knew the names were simple terms used by humans to describe "fake" creatures they thought of as hideous and terrifying, but I believed they fit beautifully.

With my first creation fully formed, I decided to awaken the life inside of it that night. I carried it deep into the woods once the eyes of every possible witness were shut. There remained a fear inside of me that anyone else who saw the child would try to destroy it, as humans do.

I placed it on the ground and knelt down. With my eyes sealed tight, I began a whisper, an incantation to the Evil One. His response was immediate and with it, my eyelids released. A reflection of my own eyes visibly formed in the sockets of my creation until they became real. My eyelids fluttered momentarily and when I stared at the silhouette in front of me, a separate soul stared back with glowing yellow eyes. My goblin was very much alive.

"My child," I whispered softly.

The small creature gave a nod and rose from the earth beneath just as I had when I entered my new form. I watched with great concentration as the goblin's awareness grew. It looked down at its arms and legs, soon realizing the potential of their mobility. It lifted a hand to the air in front of its face, a spark of curiosity emitting from its eyes. As a parent does, I sat patiently, awaiting my child to explore this act of inquiry. But almost shockingly, the goblin glanced up at me, remaining seated as I was. My prior cognition that the goblin would do as it pleased appeared to be wrong. Instead, it seemed that the young being was anticipating my permission.

With this knowledge, I rose up in the same manner. "Go on," I told the goblin.

Subsequently, the creature removed its saffron gaze from my own. It looked around momentarily, taking in its surroundings. With only seconds of observation, the goblin began to crawl similarly to a reptile, digging its claws into the soil with each step, yet it also contorted its body as if trying to slither. Moving with haste, the goblin headed towards a nearby tree. I stood in awe as the creature leaped from quite a distance and landed so perfectly on a branch, its hands and feet clinging to the bark.

The night went on with continuous observation of the goblin's agility as it pounced from tree to tree. I could not take my eyes off the wondrous life form I had created with my own hands. But, then again, I could not be praised so highly, seeing that my ability to create was simply gifted to me from one much more powerful.

I additionally learned of the creature's everlasting obedience to my words. There was not a thing I could say that it would not do. It climbed when I said climb, it ran when I said run, and it killed when I said kill. You may think of me as cruel to allow this being to harm the other living things of the forest, but it only extended its potential.

The next morning, my father questioned where I had left the goblin, although he was oblivious to its physical state. I stated plainly that I had placed it in the forest for future use in his haunted house. My father brushed past my explanation and asked me to create more of those "monsters." He said they could all be utilized as "props" in his haunted house and hopefully, they would draw more attention to the business. Needless to say, I accepted his terms and began the construction of countless other beings. I made that goblin brothers and sisters of its own species and varying others. They were all my children and they were all far more important than any treasure on the entirety of the Earth.

~ 8 ~

TUCKER

My nerves had been building for days on end. Opening night had finally arrived and I was desperate to leave school so that I had enough time to get to the haunted house. There was no way I was going to let myself or Asher be late.

Riding my bike so often to and from school had gone from one of my most hated experiences to my favorite, especially in the fall. The leaves overhead changed from green to orange right in front of my eyes. The air wasn't too cold or too hot during that time, it just brushed against your face gently like you were never meant to be anywhere else. I don't know if there was a more calming feeling than that.

When I got back to my house for a quick change of clothes, nobody else was home. It was nothing out of the ordinary, but for whatever reason, it felt more vacant that day, like my parents really had left for good. I suppose their absent tendencies screwed me up pretty badly.

Just as I grabbed my all-black attire off of my dresser, a thud sounded from my window. I froze for a second, spooked by the noise. I crept over to the window with my clothes still in hand. Suddenly, a rock pelted the tempered glass. I stepped closer, and outside, through the unkempt grass, I could see a tall figure dressed in all black. The most alarming part was the deer skull mask it was wearing. I squinted at the figure, yet it just stood completely still, staring at me from afar. I hesitantly unlocked the window and slid it open all the way.

"Hey!" I shouted.

The figure didn't move.

"Hey! What do you want?" I yelled even louder, my voice slightly cracking from the ever-building fear. I watched it without ever blinking, trying to imagine the terrifying face underneath the mask.

All of a sudden, the person began to run at a full-on sprint towards my window. I immediately slammed it shut and forced the lock back into place. At the last second, the figure slammed one of their hands forcibly against the glass and kept it there. Startled, I leaped backward, tripping over an old skateboard on my floor. My breathing was heavier than ever before as I blinked rapidly at the person outside of my house. Then, that same person began to remove the mask from their face. I can't express how relieved I felt when I saw that it was just Asher. I let out a huge sigh.

As I stood up, I could see him laughing. "Not funny, man," I voiced loudly, cracking the window open.

This only caused him to laugh more. He began stupidly

imitating my frightened expressions from only moments before.

I glared at him, sliding the window fully open. "That wasn't funny," I said again.

"Ha! Your face-" he chuckled.

I crossed my arms and leaned my head out the window, waiting for him to get over his prank.

"Dude, I don't think I've ever seen you more scared," Asher said with a grin.

I glared even more at him. "Yeah, well maybe because that's the first time I thought I was going to get murdered by some weird deer man," I said.

"Oh come on," his laughter started to fade, "I was just trying to get in the Halloween spirit."

"I don't think Ms. Farrington's going to like it if you pull that kind of stuff while we're there," I told him. I glanced down at the mask in his hands. "Where did you even get that thing?"

Asher held it up and examined it in the sunlight. "I'm not really sure. It was just lying around our house. I think my dad might've picked it up at some costume shop a couple years ago."

While Asher rambled on, I started to close the window. Just then, he placed his hand on the frame abruptly. "What are you doing?" he questioned.

"I still need to change. Your stupid prank delayed me. You better pray we're not late."

Asher rolled his eyes jokingly and made his way to the front of the house. As the sound of his steps got farther away, I slammed the window shut and gathered up my stuff.

When I got outside, Asher was already waiting on his bike. He gave me a pestering look and began to pedal away. "Let's go! You're delaying us!" he mocked.

I scowled and hopped on my bike, chasing after him.

By some miracle, Asher and I were spared from Shiloh's wrath. We managed to get to the haunted house 10 minutes early. The sun, still shining brightly in the sky, concealed all the eeriness of the property for the time being, but I knew that once it went away for the night it would be a whole different experience.

As we rode up to the parking lot, we both noticed a disturbing drawing stapled to one of the fence posts. A demented face with blank eyes stared back at us from the paper.

"Oh, well that's really comforting," Asher said sarcastically, pointing to the drawing.

That hadn't been the first time I had seen one of those creepy sketches around the property, so I wasn't too phased by it.

"So . . . where do we go?" Asher questioned, looking around the empty parking lot. "And where is everyone else?"

Just then, I barely caught a glimpse of moving silhouettes in the greenhouse. "Come on," I said to Asher, rolling my bike towards the structure.

"I already have a bad feeling about this place," Asher mumbled, trailing slowly behind me.

For a moment, I thought I heard the faint sound of

birds overhead, but I was wrong. There was nothing. I realized I had never actually seen any birds or other little creatures on that property, ever.

We laid our bikes outside of the greenhouse and approached the door. I knocked gently, the nerves causing my hands to tremble. From inside there was audible movement. Asher and I looked at each other with the same confused expression. He nodded and I knocked once more, but still, nobody answered.

"I guess we should just open it," Asher whispered.

I knew that when he said "we" he really just wanted me to do it. So, trying to keep my hand steady, I lightly pushed open the door. I peeked in and saw Shiloh busy with her work in the back.

"No need to knock, Tucker. You work here now. Remember?" she announced with her back still turned.

I entered cautiously, gesturing for Asher to come in as well. He gave me a concerned look but followed anyway. I tried to close the door as quietly as possible but the hinges still squeaked. Asher and I stood there not knowing what to say or do next.

"Go," he mouthed silently to me, tilting his head towards Shiloh.

I took a shaky breath and took a few steps forward. "U-um, Shiloh? I brought a friend with me," I stammered.

The woman stood up perfectly straight, brushed her hands gently on her black corset, and turned to face us. The glow of the sun from behind Shiloh turned her into just a dark silhouette. It was alarming how her thin shadow nearly blocked all the light as if her darkness was more powerful. I watched her take a few steps toward us in a menacing manner; each click of her heeled boots against the wood made my heart skip a beat. As she got closer, her face became more visible. Her beauty was immediately eye-catching.

I noticed Asher take a slight step back. It was apparent that Shiloh had the same intimidating effect on all people, man or woman.

"It's nice to meet you, Ms. Farrington. My name is Asher Castillo," he announced, bravely holding out his hand.

With her unbreaking gaze, the woman shook Asher's hand.

"Tucker told me about this place and thought I might be a good fit here," he added, nervously letting go of her hand.

I glanced back and forth between the two, watching their facial expressions. It was clear Asher was getting more anxious with each second that Shiloh didn't respond. But Shiloh, on the other hand, hadn't changed her cold look once.

Finally, I saw her lips begin to move. "No," she uttered plainly.

Asher and I both furrowed our brows when we heard the word leave her mouth. Shiloh wasn't bothered in the least by our surprise. She turned back around and began to work once more.

"W-wait. What do you mean? Why not?" Asher spoke up, a slight irritation in his voice.

I recoiled back, knowing his tone was noticeable and might just get him into trouble.

"No," Shiloh repeated.

Asher tilted his head. "I'm sorry, Ms. Farrington, I just don't understand," he said more softly.

I saw the stressed expression on his face and decided to chime in. "You gave me a job without really interviewing me-"

"I *did* interview you! And I interviewed him!" Shiloh yelled, spinning around to face us.

Asher and I tensed at her outburst.

"I told you, I get all the information I need simply by looking at a person. There would be no good reason to sit down with every ignorant individual who appears on my doorstep and delve into the most ridiculous parts of their lives of which I *do not* particularly care about. My answer is no. I do not think you would be a good fit here nor do I need you to continue distracting me from my work. Good day, Asher," the woman said fiercely.

Asher began to walk towards the door. I tried to make him wait a moment longer, but he shoved past me and went right outside. I glanced back at Shiloh, but she was unphased.

Just as I was about to follow my friend, I heard Shiloh say my name.

"Tucker," she voiced calmly.

"Yes?"

"Don't bring that boy back in here. Or any of your other acquaintances. None of them belong," Shiloh stated.

I nodded nervously.

"Oh, and don't be gone too long. We have much to prepare for," she added. Her voice seemed to echo through the structure, which was impossible, and yet, I felt the vibration through the floor.

I raced out the door to catch up with Asher. By the time I got outside, he was already at the road on his bike.

"Asher!" I called, running towards him.

He looked back at me and rolled his eyes. I expected him to just ride off anyway and ignore me, but instead, he placed a foot on the ground and waited.

"I'm sorry, man. I had no idea she would react like that," I said, catching my breath.

Asher let out a disgruntled sigh. "I told you she's a freak. I mean what the hell was that? She just shakes my hand and knows that she hates me? How does that make sense?" he griped.

"It doesn't," I shook my head, "But everything she does is odd. She owns a haunted house, dude. I mean, from what I've seen . . . I feel like she might be some kind of witch or something."

"Are you insane?" Asher's voice grew louder. He scowled and began to shake his head. "You think she's a witch and you wanna stick around this place?"

"Well I don't know if she really is one, I-I just have seen her do some crazy stuff that I've never seen before," I explained.

Asher shook his head even more, clearly not wanting to hear me spew any more bullshit.

"She probably just has practice with illusions and stuff," I rambled, realizing how crazy I sounded.

"Dude, that woman is tricking you! Something is *not* right about this place!"

"So you believe all those stupid rumors people made up?" I interrogated, gradually matching Asher's irritation.

"What else am I supposed to believe? So far, it seems like they were all right." There was concern in his eyes. He cared, but he showed it like a protective older brother would, and that got on my nerves.

"Fine. Then just go. I'll figure it out myself without some narrow-minded opinion that the rest of you have," I asserted harshly.

Asher seemed taken aback. He looked at me with a hurt frown and got back on his bike.

Before I could even comprehend the argument, Asher was already far down the road. His figure turned into just a tiny dot in the distance. I felt instant regret and stared at the dusty ground. I kicked at the dirt and lifted my head to see the disaster I had gotten myself into. I was surrounded on all sides by a new world full of terrifying wonders that I couldn't escape, at least not until I figured out the truth.

~ 9 ~

METSAH

The vibrance of the seasons fluctuated throughout time, although my work did not. In the colder months, I dedicated my time to the collection of ideas and substances for my future children, and in the warmer months, I would mend their bodies until they were ready to be given life. I did not regret a single moment of the time I spent on them, no matter how frustrating or tiresome it may have been. That forest was soon filled with creatures tall and tiny, strong and slender, brooding and brilliant. I ensured that they were tucked away safely in the trees, out of sight from any dangers of the disgraceful world that belonged to humanity.

My father – the horrendous fool – never questioned my capabilities or those of my children because I limited his perception, only allowing him to see what I wanted him to see. Not to mention, he was utterly blinded by the massive growth rate of success his business undertook once I became involved. Each new customer he gained was due to me. As another gift, I was given the knowledge of flamboyance and the bizarre, a useful tool in the realm of haunted houses. Amongst the ghouls and beasts, I also created visual wonders through structures. My talents were put into specialized pieces that worked like hypnosis. I utilized these traits of mine in ways that an average being might view as unthinkable, and yet, this is what drew people to the business. They admired the unusual, but they also feared it. Hypocrites. My father was just like them. So brainless, so ignorant, so . . . pointless.

While I worked endlessly, he spent his nights getting drunk, no, not drunk with sorrow, but drunk with happiness. He was a disgrace, joyful or sad. In his own delusional method, he convinced himself that he was the very cause of his success. I was simply bound to work in the shadows as he clawed at the recognition.

With time, I grew tired of the man's valiant efforts to claim power over the haunted house and my patience was running thin. All it would take was one more slight push and I would tumble off into an abyss of uncontrollable fury. Upon my return from that pit, I would bring the fires of Hell along with me.

Unfortunately for my father, he never wisened up, and his actions sent me plunging off that cliff with the utmost force. You see, I was busy with one of my most beautiful creations yet and it took all of my restrained focus to accomplish the outcome I was hoping for. I had kept the door to the greenhouse shut for this specific reason; the slightest inconvenience would be perilous. I had only needed a few more hours of work before it would be complete, but that was when my father brazenly invited himself inside the structure. My composure, already coming to its end, was alerted to me upon the man's entrance. I gave him no acknowledgment as he obnoxiously hovered nearby. There were no words that came from his mouth, yet I could feel the imbecilic critiques in his silence. I could sense his eyes on the face of my creation, judging it with no remorse. Surely, a dull comment would be made soon enough.

Aligning perfectly with my presumption, the man just had to open his mouth. "Can you hurry this up?" my father asked. His tone was blatantly disrespectful. He could no longer even use the name of his own daughter. I had become just a worker bee to him, a nameless, faceless, little insect that was so far beneath him and all his riches.

"No," I responded, continuing to attach layers of fur.

The man huffed with his arms crossed like a child. "I need it done soon. A couple of guys offered to do an advertisement for us and I want to make sure this *thing* is seen in it," he said.

I had to force myself to take an extra breath to compensate for his insolence towards my creation. "One cannot rush perfection," I told him. Now, I believed that I had extended my patience even further than the man deserved at that point, which was quite generous on my behalf. But he kept on pushing.

"You finished the others so quickly. Why is this one taking so long? Isn't it just a bunch of wood and fake fur you're gluing together?" my father continued.

At that time I could no longer tell if he was purely

that unintelligent or if he really was trying to antagonize me. The one thing I was sure of was my absolute hatred for him. "Fine!" I lobbed the fur onto the ground. "If you want it to be done so badly, then I will make it done!" I bellowed.

The man stepped back and threw his hands in the air the way one does when accused of something they know they are guilty of. "W-well hold on a second now-" he stammered.

I thrust my hand into the chest of my creation where the heart would be. I shut my eyes tight and generated every bit of power I could muster.

My father cowered in the corner. His fear kept him from being able to leave; it worked to my advantage quite well.

In seconds, my eyelids opened, and in front of me appeared the blood-red eyes of my newest child. I released my hand from its chest and turned to my father. He had fallen silent, mesmerized by terror. Without his voice, he had no strength at all. He was a true coward.

"It is done. Enjoy," I announced.

With one last glimpse of his pitiful face, I stepped out of the greenhouse, shutting the door behind me. I barred it immediately, knowing the man would likely make one last futile attempt at escape . . . and he did. I turned my back to the structure while he brutally slammed his fists on the door. His shrieks and wails of pain only gave me satisfaction.

I believe my remorse for humanity died that day. I

realized just how tiresome and completely unnecessary they were.

Once the man's cries finally died out, I turned back around. Seeping from the undercut of the door was the thick, distinct, red liquid. I lifted the slab of wood that kept the door sealed and gently pushed, allowing my child to have its first breath of home. A deep growl sounded from inside. I widened the opening as an invitation out of the structure.

The extraordinary wolf-like beast filled the entire doorway with its shoulders alone. It stood on two muscular legs that easily gave it four feet of height, making it taller than the frame of the door. Its fur was dark and full, yet patchy in areas, revealing the bones underneath, including most of its face, which was the result of my father's interruption. Although, I may consider giving him that slight credit as well because the unfinished, "ugly" result was even more perfect in my eyes.

I listened to the great power of its lungs as it inhaled the open air. Closer and closer it approached, walking on all four paws, although the front ones were more similarly representative of hands.

"My child," I whispered.

I noticed the creature's ears perk up, even at the faint sound of my voice. It looked at me intently like they all did when they were born. A young, speculative beauty ready to learn. We maintained allegiant eye contact as the beast got as close as possible. Just then, it got up on two legs again, easily standing at eight feet tall. It stared down at me. Although I was beneath the creature by technicality, it recognized that it answered to me, and me alone. With a meek head tilt, the creature held out a hand, careful to mind the jaggedness of its claws. I accepted the obedient gesture and placed my hand in its own.

I soon came to the realization that the responsibility of naming these creations was now resting on my shoulders. I stared into the beast's eyes for a moment longer, searching the depths of its individuality.

Finally, a name of perfection came to my mind. "Keres," I said.

The beast nodded in recognition, accepting its given name.

"Go, my love. Explore your home," I commanded softly with the touch of a mother's voice.

The creature released my hand gently and took off in the most opposite manner with movements so violent and untamed. I adored its behaviors just as I did all my other children's. I observed the new creation disappear into the woods and an uproar of joyous howls broke out when it met its brothers and sisters.

I returned my attention to the greenhouse as I was reminded of the man's corpse due to the repulsive stench that always flowed off of humans when they died. When I looked down at his pathetic body I couldn't help but smirk. There was no greater pleasure than accomplishing exactly what I was put on Earth to do. I dragged the lifeless body out of the greenhouse and neatly left it within the forest's edge for my children to consume when they preferred.

~ 10 ~

TUCKER

The sun blazed on the ground, giving us a little bit of heat before the chill of night kicked in. The property still remained vacant, except for the odd sounds that always came from the woods.

For over an hour, I trudged back and forth from the barn to the dirt lot, carrying lights, simple Halloween decorations, and boxes of tickets for the customers. Every once in a while I caught a glimpse of Anthony lurking nearby, usually from inside the barn. His face always had the same terrified expression. Somehow, he was looking worse than usual. I never had a chance to speak to him, but I got the feeling it was for the best.

I had taken a five-minute break in the greenhouse to calm myself as the nerves ramped up. "It's all going well," I huffed. I had to keep telling myself that every once in a while or else I wouldn't be able to get a clear thought out.

I was bringing the final box over when my jaw dropped in shock. Right where I had witnessed an open lot of dirt only minutes ago, there were now multiple concession stands, a ticket booth, a mini stage, and wooden poles that were strung with all the lights I had just brought. The ground was littered with pumpkins, some carved, some not. I had never even seen any pumpkins on the property before so I had no idea where they could have come from so spontaneously. Classic monster cutouts were placed all over, their goofy, cartoon faces smiling at me. With all the brilliant colors and details, it looked like the entrance to a spooky carnival.

I stepped through the entrancing scene until I found Shiloh standing right in the center of it all. She was gracefully balanced on a step ladder in her heeled boots, attaching one last strand of purple lights overhead.

"Shiloh, how did you get all of this up so quickly? And on your own . . ." I trailed off, noticing more and more decorations everywhere I looked.

"It's a little talent I have," she responded casually, stepping onto the ground.

"Seems like you have a lot of those," I mumbled under my breath.

The woman acted like none of it was strange as she brushed past me. "Come along, Tucker. I need you to do one last thing before we open," she said.

I followed her back to the greenhouse, growing increasingly anxious as the time to open got closer. Shiloh pushed the door open hastily and told me to wait outside. I kicked at the pebbles under my feet, arranging them into terrified faces that matched my own internal feelings. She returned with multiple bundles of rope in hand. I can easily say that my fear spiked when I saw it.

"What's that?" I spoke up without hesitation.

"I need you to set this up along both sides of the trail. Sometimes people get a bit . . . *confused* and wander off into the trees. And trust me, nothing good happens when they leave the trail. I'd prefer to keep them as contained as possible," Shiloh explained.

"Oh."

"Here," she said, handing me the rope.

I nearly dropped it, surprised by how heavy it actually was. I scrambled to keep it from unraveling while also trying to keep up with Shiloh's fast-paced walk.

We got to the entrance of the forest and like usual, the uneasy feeling returned. It was one thing having someone with me while I was there, but being told to go alone, well, that was just a heart attack waiting to happen.

"Just tie it to any of the trees nearest to the trail. There are plenty of them," she said, almost humorously.

"Alright," I answered confidently, trying to hide the shakiness in my vocal cords.

Shiloh turned and began to walk back. "Return to the greenhouse when you've finished," she ordered.

My hesitance to enter the woods was suddenly overcome when I looked past the trees and saw the warm glow of sunlight peeking through. Much like the first time I ever saw it, I was immediately drawn in. Even the gargoyles didn't seem to have an effect on me.

I tied the first end of the rope to a tree and walked smoothly down the path, my body finally relaxed. As I went, I noticed how serene everything seemed. The leaves were perfectly still, the sun's light didn't waver, and there was no noise whatsoever. I stopped to tie off the other end of the first rope and realized just how quiet it really was. The silence was slowly becoming eerie. I glanced up, suddenly getting the feeling that there were eyes on me. I looked all around but didn't get a glimpse of anything or anyone. I knew Soul of the Wilderness was a weird place, but Asher was right, there was definitely something incredibly strange about it that set it apart from any other experience I ever had.

Just as I was tying the last piece of rope, a loud rustle sounded from the brush a few feet away from me. My head shot up and my eyes searched the area where I heard it. Suddenly, I felt a cold sweat form on my forehead. Of course, something just had to happen in my final minutes of being there. I couldn't just get through without getting spooked by something.

But when I checked, all I saw were the usual shapes of the trees. I decided I was just being paranoid and made my way back to the greenhouse like Shiloh said. By then, the sun was nearly set and the lights from the front were glowing even brighter. I was in a hurry to get inside as the dusk air chilled my skin.

"Ah, good," Shiloh said when I entered the greenhouse. She immediately handed me a puffy black jacket with the word: **SECURITY** printed on the back in bold white letters. "This now belongs to you," she stated firmly.

I put the jacket on and the goosebumps from the cold immediately disappeared.

"You'll find a flashlight, a blade, and a set of keys in the pockets there," Shiloh pointed to the coat, "Do your best not to lose any of those materials. Rest assured we will be able to find them again, but it can be a bit of a hassle."

I rummaged through the pockets, identifying each of the items and remembering their locations just in case I needed them. I will say I was a little surprised that Shiloh just willingly gave me a knife considering I was just some random teenager, but I guess that according to her, I wasn't so random at all.

Shiloh observed me for a moment longer, almost like how a mother would look at her son on his first day of school. "Oh, and lastly," she said, pulling something from her shirt pocket. It turned out to be a necklace of sorts with a leather cord and a golden snake with emerald-green eyes. "I'll need you to keep this on at all times during the night," she said, gently handing me the necklace.

As I put it around my neck, I realized that the snake pendant was the same as the ring Shiloh always wore. I convinced myself that it was probably just a symbol of the haunted house and all the employees had to wear one. And then I also realized that I was still yet to see another employee besides Anthony.

"Where is everyone else?" I asked her, fiddling with the snake around my neck.

"They're already in their places," the woman responded.

She casually led me outside and gazed towards the trees. From afar, we could hear the audible howls and groans that always seemed to echo from that forest. I couldn't understand how all the actors got in there without me seeing a single one of them. You probably think I'm stupid for saying that, but at the time I truly couldn't wrap my head around it.

"Ah, looks like everyone at the front is ready as well," Shiloh said happily, looking over at the area with all the booths and entertainment.

I glanced past her, once again, my mind filled with shock. For the first time since being there, I saw some of the other employees.

On the little spotlit stage stood a man with his hands tightly wrapped around a microphone stand. He was dressed in a pair of black slacks and dress shoes, along with an overly eccentric red coat. He had a funny-looking, striped tophat on his head that cast a shadow over half of his face. I squinted, trying to get a better look at him when suddenly, he turned only his head towards me while his body remained facing the front of the stage. My heart skipped a beat when I saw the deranged smile he had under layers of intricate clown makeup. I assumed he must have been wearing costume contacts as well because even from the shadow of his hat I could see his piercing white eyes with a tiny black pupil in the center. His smile seemed to get wider and wider, looking less human by the second.

I looked away shortly, unable to withstand the gaze of his eyes. Even after I looked away, I could still feel him watching me and I could still sense that undaunting smile smiling at me.

Then, in the concession stands and ticket booth, I

caught quick glimpses of people also dressed up in strange costumes. From what I could tell, they just seemed like normal people, especially when compared to the freak on the stage. But I guess that's kind of what I signed up to be surrounded by: freaks.

I also noticed the dozens of cars pulling into the dirt lot, their headlights blinding us all as they parked. They seemed frantic to get as close to the front as possible. This haunted house really was as popular as the news portrayed it to be.

"I'd like you to start heading over," Shiloh told me, gesturing towards the woods.

I gulped. "Okay. A-and what is it that you need me to do while I'm there?" I asked, knowing I couldn't hide the stutter.

"Just walk the perimeter and make sure everything is running smoothly. But do *not* enter. Do you understand?" she stated.

I nodded.

"If there is any trouble I will know. You leave them be and let me handle it. I know how to calm them down," Shiloh muttered, gazing longingly in the direction of the forest. "Alright?"

I nodded again and hesitantly began walking down the path. Only a few steps in, I glanced back. Shiloh was gone. She must have already gone to the front to welcome everyone in.

I took my time getting to the forest, especially since I was just on patrol duty. At first, I was a bit more calm than usual because there were no strange noises, but then it hit me; *there were no strange noises.* Only moments ago there were all sorts of sounds and now there was nothing at all?

My eyes remained wide open as I slowly walked the edge of the forest. I stared deeply into the darkness, but the only thing I could see were the lanterns that hung along the trail. I could see their warm glow lighting up the surrounding trees and every once in a while I imagined terrifying faces that were completely made up by my own mind. I think I was more disturbed that I didn't actually see any of the actors.

All of a sudden, an uproar of voices sounded from a distance. I stopped and watched large groups of people heading towards the entrance. They were laughing and goofing around up until they got to the wooden arch with the gargoyles. I could make out some of their expressions and they were no longer smiling. I took a few steps closer and finally saw what they were all staring at, and surprisingly, it wasn't the looming gargoyles. Under the arch stood a figure, an oddly shaped being that appeared to be made entirely out of wood. It looked like it had physically come from the arch itself because its entire backside, from head to toe, was sporadically broken into sharp ends.

Just then, a person in one of the groups spoke to the being. "Can we go in?" they asked.

The wooden figure nodded and moved slightly to the side, allowing them to pass through. Only one group was able to enter before the being stepped in front again, blocking the entrance. For a split second, as the figure was turning back, I caught a glimpse of its face. It had bright yellow, glowing eyes that illuminated everything around it like there was a lantern within its head. Besides the eyes, it had no other facial features whatsoever. I could only help but wonder how the person breathed – if it was a person at all.

I stayed in that spot for a long time, watching the odd behavior of this being at the entrance and how it interacted with the customers. Every minute or so, it would let the next group in, keeping a consistent spacing between each one. It was amusing to watch the people enter the forest with all their mixed reactions. The groups of teenagers would typically start to scream immediately, claiming to see things that nobody else could. Then, there were the groups of adults. Half of them were drunk and could barely walk, making me wonder why Shiloh even let them in. And then, there were the boring ones; they didn't seem to have any fun at all. They were the types of people who were so horror-obsessed that nothing ever phased them anymore. There were also the people who brought in young children; they were the dumbest. Their kids would start crying before they even entered. Lastly, we had the groups of "haunt professionals." they got on my nerves the most with the way they sauntered through like the arrogant jerks they were, critiquing every little aspect they could since they felt they knew better. As the night went on, and I got to experience more of peoples' behavior, I started to understand why Shiloh dealt with them the way she did. After years of being in this business, it must have gotten tiring to put up with all their crap.

Eventually, I realized I wasn't really keeping up with the job I was assigned to, so I began to walk the perimeter once more. The temperature was fairly tolerable up until the wind began to pick up, then it became frigid. I could feel the tip of my nose going numb the longer I was out there. The breeze also began to draw in clouds, covering the stars in the sky, and separating me from the rest of the world. I kept a slow pace as I walked, branches and fallen leaves crunching under my shoes. For what felt like forever, I listened to the terrified screams of the customers and the horrific howls and groans that the actors somehow managed to make. For a while, it all just seemed like the normal kind of stuff that went on at a haunted house, but then, I was reminded of how abnormal this place really was.

I was towards the very back of the woods, farthest from all of civilization, when I saw a massive, dark figure shifting in the trees nearby. I froze in place, trying not to make a noise. I couldn't believe how unnaturally tall and broad-shouldered the figure was. I assumed that they must have been wearing stilts under a heavy costume made of fur, but that assumption didn't last long. The way it moved so smoothly with all of its hulking features was too perfect to be just a costume. I didn't know what to think.

Then, I made the mistake of exhaling slightly too loudly. It clearly caught the creature's attention because I saw its ear twitch at the sound. I had never felt a fear so intense within myself like I did in that moment. The creature tilted its head back towards me and revealed a pair of blood-red eyes. They were so illuminated that the red hue hit my face through the slight spaces between the trees. The beast began to shift in its position and turn the rest of its body towards me as well. That's when I knew that these "actors" were not actually human. I remained still, thinking that there was no point in running because I would be dead in a matter of seconds. The creature snarled, releasing a deep, throaty growl that I could feel in my chest. It bared its jagged teeth and flexed the claws of its gigantic hands. Just when I thought it was about to tear into me, it noticed the pendant around my neck and appeared to grimace. Baffled and close to passing out, I watched the creature turn and disappear deeper into the woods like it never saw me.

Finally, when the beast was no longer in sight, I allowed myself to breathe again. My chest heaved with fear. I tried to comprehend everything I just experienced, which even made me question my own sanity. Was any of it real? Was I hallucinating? Was my whole time at this "haunted house" just a dream or some terrible nightmare? I mean, to put it in simple terms, I had just seen a werewolf, or at least some demented, altered form of a werewolf.

I quickly pulled out my phone and checked the time. It was 11 o'clock. I just had to wait one more hour before I was free to go, that was if I could even survive that long.

I spent the rest of the time pacing as slowly as possible around the woods, not wanting to draw any more attention to myself, and made a point of keeping a firm grasp on the knife in my pocket in case of another encounter. I kept going over the thought of there being a slim chance that what I had seen was purely just an overly perfect costume, but then I pictured those eyes, those horrible red eyes. Everywhere I looked I saw them. My imagination was starting to easily get to me just like Shiloh had said.

After a few minutes of no longer hearing any screams or voices, I whipped out my phone. Midnight. I was ready to dart out of there at full speed. I slipped my phone back into my pocket and walked as quickly as I physically could towards the greenhouse, fully bypassing the entrance of the woods. Once I got on that path towards safety I didn't look back.

"Shiloh! Shiloh!" I shouted as I neared the ticket booth. I swiveled around in the dirt, searching rampantly for her.

Suddenly, a cold hand touched my shoulder. I spun around and saw Shiloh standing there perfectly calm. "Tucker," she acknowledged.

My panicked breathing obviously told her something was going on with me. I tried to stop it, but I couldn't. My instincts kept pumping adrenaline throughout my whole body.

"What's wrong?" she asked in that disturbingly serene tone. She still looked as perfect as when I saw her at the beginning of the night, and then there was myself, who was like a rabid, forest child who just saw discovered society.

"Is it over? Is the night over? Can I go home now?" I said frantically.

The woman intertwined her fingers. "Yes, the night is over and I would say it turned out rather well," she stated, observing the now quiet property. She then looked back at me, almost in a judging manner. "Tell me what ails your mind, boy," Shiloh said coolly.

I scrunched up my hands in my pockets, trying to gain the confidence to speak the truth about what I had seen. As I glanced down at the ground, I could feel her gaze pouring into me. She tilted her head slightly, demanding a response.

"I hope they didn't frighten you too much. I'll admit they may appear quite intimidating at first, but as you have seen, they mean no harm," Shiloh added.

Her words struck a nerve in my brain and I immediately looked back up at her. "'Frighten' is an understatement," I muttered.

She raised her eyebrows.

"Why don't you just tell me what the hell is really going on here? I mean, you're really going to tell me that those things in that forest are just actors?" I said, unable to find my usual sense of respect.

Her expression changed and I could see the very moment that she lost her patience. "I told you, I molded each one of them into perfection, Tucker. They behave how I tell them to, which means they *act* as ferocious, frightening beasts. Do you know where you are? Do you understand what you signed up for? At night, when the trees come to life, and everything normal about society is shut out, you are not meant to feel comfortable. That is a false hope that you must lose. Don't play the fool, boy. You welcomed the darkness, so now you're getting the darkness," the woman scolded.

As harsh as they were, her words felt honest, like she was trying to knock some sense into me about reality. But I wish I had known that they weren't reality at all, they were one of the various forms of manipulation. Yet, of course, I was naive, in desperate need of money, and found those pieces of my sister in Shiloh, so I accepted her explanation at face value.

She wasn't pleased with me and I had no idea how to fix it. Even when I handed the necklace back to her she kept her viperous look.

I went home that night with plenty of money in my pocket and no sense in the world of how I was tricked.

TUCKER

I hoped Shiloh's explanation would have allowed me to sleep that night, but it did not. My mind was restless as the memories of the werewolf encounter continued to appear. I tossed and turned for hours, but flashes of the beast's red eyes kept popping into my head. Even if it was just a costume, there was something so unnatural about them. I could tell they had evil intent; they were looking for someone to harm, and I just happened to not be the right fit.

Eventually, after saying some prayers to get the horrible image out of my head, I was able to fall asleep around four in the morning. I slept for a few solid hours until I was suddenly woken up by shouting from outside my door. My parents were arguing over something. I assumed it was probably money-related, though I didn't care to listen. I had heard enough of their extensive fighting over the years and I no longer had the energy for it. My desire to leave that house was growing stronger each day. At least that's one thing we agreed on: I wanted out and they wanted me out as well.

Unable to go back to sleep, I got myself dressed and planned on just waiting in my room until the arguing died down, but then, I got a loud knock on my door. Before the person even said anything, I could sense I was going to get yelled at for no good reason. There was never a good reason.

"Tucker! Get your ass out here!" my father's deep voice bellowed.

I rolled off my bed and lumpishly walked to the door. The man's fist was already in the air, ready to bang on the door once more by the time I opened it. I just looked at him plainly, not even saying anything because I knew he wasn't going to let me get a word in.

"Where were you last night?" he asked, glaring furiously.

"I was working," I said calmly.

He gave an angry glance at my mom and then turned back to me. "And you didn't care to tell us?" His voice began to grow louder as he stepped closer. His movements were almost violent, as was the look on his face.

I kept my gaze level with his, trying not to let him intimidate me. "I didn't think you cared. You hardly ask about my life as it is."

That was a mistake. I immediately regretted what I said because then my mom decided to join in.

"Oh, so you're saying we don't fucking care about you? Is that it?" she said loudly, placing her hands on her hips with that angry mom hunch.

I knew it would be better to bite my tongue than give the snarky answer I had prepared in my head. My parents continued to glare at me, waiting impatiently for me to respond. My eyes shifted back and forth between them, my mind running blank on what to say.

"I don't know," I finally voiced. I shoved past my dad and went to the kitchen. Luckily, I was able to escape for a moment as they started bickering with each other again, swearing and all.

I grabbed a snack and flopped down on the couch in the living room. My parents began to move their argument toward me so I switched on the TV and turned it up to nearly full volume. Almost as if they knew their voices agitated me, they began to get louder. I tried to turn up the volume even more but at a certain point, it couldn't go any higher. I flipped through the stations, trying to find whatever would block them out the most.

Just then, a local news story popped up about our town. I paused and sat upright, trying to focus on the report. It claimed there had been an attack in the night from an unknown animal and that a young woman was brutally killed. They showed blurred images of the woman's mangled body lying by the side of the road. My eyes grew wider as they went into detail about the woman's previous whereabouts. They claimed she had visited Soul of the Wilderness that night and she was never seen after that. I immediately thought back to the creature I had encountered, visualizing its gigantic claws brutally tearing at the woman. I shook my head, trying to get the image out of my mind. I didn't want to come to any hasty conclusion based on random events that might have no connection whatsoever. In fact, maybe the gigantic beast I saw was just a bear. Maybe this was just a bear attack (at least that's what I tried to convince myself of).

"Tucker, we need to talk about this job of yours," my dad suddenly voiced.

"Wait," I put up my hand instantly. I wanted to hear the rest of the story, no matter what the consequences would be for talking back.

I could feel my father's enraged gaze on the back of my head, but he remained quiet, also taking an interest in the news story.

Most of the same information was repeated as we listened. I was just about to turn it off when suddenly, an interview with a local man popped up. I furrowed my brow, feeling like I recognized him somehow. As I watched his stern movements and bitter facial expressions, I realized it was the bar owner who worked next to Shiloh's property. The reporter questioned him about any suspicious activity he might have seen, but the man began to go into a full-on rave about his dislike for Shiloh instead.

"It was her! I know it was Shiloh Farrington!" he yelled in a strong Spanish accent. He kept his arms tightly folded over his chest in an irritated manner. "That girl has been nothing but trouble. Her freak show has driven so many people away from my business. So many! I'm telling you, she is working alongside the Devil. There is no other explanation. After all, she killed her own family. What makes you think she wouldn't kill a random woman?" the man rambled on. His words got faster and faster as he spoke, eventually becoming a jumbled, incoherent mess.

"Ah, this guy's just another loon," my dad said, ripping the remote from my hands and shutting off the TV.

I sat back for a moment, only focused on what the man had said about Shiloh.

"Damn it, Tucker!" my mom shouted.

I turned to see both of my parents giving me that look again.

"You're going to tell us about this job of yours," my mom demanded.

I hesitated, but there was no use in lying. "I work there," I pointed to the TV, "At the haunted house."

The two of them exchanged wide-eyed glares.

"You got yourself involved with a fucking murderer? How fucking stupid are you, boy?" my dad shouted.

I stood up irately. "I thought you didn't even believe that stuff! You just called that guy a loon for saying it!"

"Don't raise your voice at me, you little shit," he growled, stepping closer with clenched fists.

I didn't budge. And to this day I still remember feeling my self-control slip away from me. "You don't even know what you're talking about! She is not a murderer! People like you are just so dumb that they'll believe anything they hear!" I shouted with all the built-up fervor I had in me.

I couldn't tell you exactly what happened after I said those things. All I know is that I woke up later that day in the middle of the floor with a puffy, black ring around my eye. It hadn't been the first time, and I knew they wouldn't let it be the last.

There was still time left in the day before I had to work and I sure wasn't going to spend it in that house. I grabbed all the stuff I needed and left without ever wondering or caring where my parents had gone. And clearly, proving my point, they didn't care where I went either. They just wanted to cause problems when there weren't any.

My bike was outside in the sunshine, ready to go, almost as if it had been waiting impatiently to rescue me.

It didn't take long for me to realize that I hadn't been the greatest friend to Asher and Charli ever since getting the job. I had left them without much explanation of anything in my life for the past few days and I felt an overwhelming amount of guilt. I sent them both a text, asking if they would meet me at the abandoned church. Charli agreed before I even left my house. I suppose she didn't have as much reason to dislike me as Asher did. He didn't even respond. I just had to hope that he would show up, and knowing him, he would. That's one of the things we all loved about him; no matter how angry he might've been, he always showed up for his friends.

When I arrived at the church, neither of them were anywhere to be seen. I leaned my bike against the rickety building and clambered through one of the windows. All of a sudden, two hands appeared in front of my face and a female scream rang through my ears. I tumbled to the ground, landing right on my shoulder. My hands and feet scurried around on the dusty floor as I tried to back away. I scrambled to get up, blood rushing through my veins. That's when I saw Charli standing over me with her hands on her hips. She had one of those mastered, emotionless looks on her face as usual.

"Look who it is," she said plainly. Her eyes traveled across my face until she got to my black eye. "What happened there?" she pointed to it.

I gave her a knowing glance and she immediately understood.

"Assholes," she muttered under her breath.

"I swear you people are trying to give me a heart attack," I huffed. I wiped the dirt off my clothes and looked out the window. "Is Asher coming?"

"No clue. He told me about your job," Charli said, taking a seat on one of the old pews.

Out of the corner of my eye, I could see Charli glaring at me. I had a feeling that whatever Asher had told her wasn't positive. I sighed and sat down in the row across from her.

She tilted her head at me but said nothing. Charli did this often. She would just sit and take a moment to observe the person in front of her. It always made the other person uncomfortable because they believed she was judging them, but she was simply studying, breaking down character. I'll admit that I became stressed every time she did this to me. I felt like she would see something negative in me that even I couldn't see.

"What?" I finally spoke up.

Charli grinned. "I was right, wasn't I? That place is screwed up," she stated confidently.

I looked down in partial shame. My friends were right

and I knew that, but half of me still had a strong urge to defend it.

"Asher said the woman's a witch," Charli added.

"She's just . . . odd. I don't know. So much has happened that it's hard to put it all together."

"Like what? What happened, Tucker?" She leaned over and rested her elbows on her knees, looking at me intensely.

My mind knew what to say but I couldn't get the words out properly. "I guess he's not too far off by calling her a witch. It's like she uses some sort of magic but-"

Just then, we were both surprised to see Asher crawling through the window opening. Charli laughed as he hit his head on the frame.

"Shut up," he scowled at her.

She continued to laugh, making fun of him like siblings would. "Ha! Maybe you shouldn't walk around like such a lumbering idiot."

"Maybe you should keep your mouth shut," he mocked back.

The two glared at each other in a ridiculing manner until Asher looked at me. His anger from the previous day still resonated in his eyes.

"I guess I'll just bud out of this," Charli mumbled, raising her eyebrows. Her comment only made things more uncomfortable but she enjoyed our discomfort.

Silence filled the tiny building. My brain was screaming at me to say something, but my voice felt so weak. My eyes wandered all around, finally landing on my fidgeting hands. "I'm still alive," I said calmly.

"I see that," Asher responded in the same tone.

We stared at each other with resentment for a moment longer. Charli folded her arms tensely in the background like she was watching a movie.

"But I was wrong," I dropped my head, "And I'm sorry I didn't listen to you."

"Finally," Charli murmured, dropping her shoulders.

Asher and I both shot her an irritated glance. She gave us a goofy grin and turned her head away.

"Tucker, you've got to realize that we're just looking out for you. I didn't get a good vibe from that place, and I know you didn't either," Asher furrowed his brow sympathetically. His tone was kind, which I appreciated. "And if the rumors are true . . . a-and that woman really is working with some sort of dark power, then I don't want you to have any sort of involvement with her. That's like being an accomplice to the Devil," he said sincerely.

I didn't hesitate to speak the first thought that came to my mind. No evil was going to stop me. "I think the rumors are true," I blurted out.

Asher and Charli both gave me the same wild look. For a moment, nobody spoke. We sat there, all unanimously shocked by what I had said. I could feel a sort of guilt inside me that I couldn't even explain. It was like I was being punished for trying to tell them the truth.

"What do you mean, Tucker?" Asher spoke up. His eyes were brimming with dread.

My eyes shifted between the two of them, the guilt was turning into a burning pain. It was like a hot rod was being pressed into my heart. I folded my arms over my chest, trying to suppress it. I couldn't tell if the pain was really there or not.

"Tucker," Charli said softly.

I gulped nervously, worried that the pain would grow. "I think . . . there is something evil in that forest. I've seen all the costumes and props that are made there and they just aren't right. I feel like they're always watching me everywhere I go. Shiloh says it's just a bunch of actors, but-"

Suddenly, the pain in my chest struck me like a knife. I twisted uncomfortably in my seat. The discomfort on my face was obvious.

"Are you okay?" Charli asked immediately, leaning towards me.

"I'm fine," I nodded. I forced myself to sit upright as the twinge faded away.

Asher folded his arms socratically, clearly going over my explanation silently in his head.

"I don't think it's a good idea to keep working there. You're putting yourself in danger," Charli told me.

When she said the word "danger" I instantly thought of the news report from earlier that day. I wanted to tell them, but again, that phantom ache started to return.

"She's right," Asher glanced at us both, "You need to quit before things get out of your control."

"I'd say they're already out of my control. She has total power over that forest. I don't know how or why, but she does. And I'm not disagreeing with you guys, I know I need to quit. But first, I want to figure out what's going on there. I want people to see the truth."

Asher and Charli glanced at each other and then back at me.

"How are you gonna do that?" Charli questioned.

"I'm not sure."

Once again, Asher seemed deep in thought. We watched him pace the small area for a minute or so until he finally stopped. "Ms. Farrington trusts you, doesn't she?" he asked.

"Yeah, I'd say so." The guilt was creeping up in the back of my mind again. I didn't like where any of this was going.

"So, potentially, you could sneak around the property for a little bit and try to find something. Use her trust to your advantage while it lasts," Asher explained.

"Yeah, and maybe you could even get some photos of the demented stuff she's got in that place," Charli added.

The two of them became overly enthusiastic about the idea very quickly. I felt that strong urge to defend Shiloh and the haunted house itself. My friends went on and on, describing their plan in depth.

The more they spoke, the more I felt an uncontrollable anger taking over and I suddenly shouted, "No!"

They both looked at me in bewilderment. I had the same reaction as them. Why was I so mad all of a sudden? What was going on inside of me?

"No," I repeated much more quietly. I shifted uncomfortably in my seat from the arisen tension. "We're not going to make any rash decisions. I don't want to accuse Shiloh of something that might not even be true," I told them.

Asher took a step closer to me, almost aggressively. "Tucker, you just said that you know she's working with something supernatural. And now you want to keep pretending things are perfectly normal? You're contradicting yourself."

My mind was running blank. I had no idea why I just defended Shiloh. It was like something else was partially controlling my mind.

"Innocent until proven guilty I guess," Charli chimed in.

"Exactly," I commented, staring at Asher. "I work tonight too, so I'll see if anything weird happens."

He stared back begrudgingly. "Fine. But you have to tell us everything. You can't leave out any details," he said in an almost threatening manner. "And if there are any signs of danger," he made direct eye contact, "Then you *have* to leave. Got it?"

"Fine," I said, replicating his same broodish energy.

After our dissatisfied agreement, the three of us parted ways. Asher and Charli returned home, while I went straight to the haunted house.

~ 12 ~

METSAH

In the time before I was imprisoned to the confines of the trees, I walked the land as any other woman. Although, my freedom was limited due to the predominant nature of men. They failed to show us the fundamental respect that one deserves for simply upholding the essence of a human. I suppose this may have begun the hatred in my heart and the reasoning for what I did, for what I did to myself and to all of them. And yet, I stand firm in the decision I made with nil remorse. Those loathsome creatures deserved what they got and now they will burn just as I have been sentenced to.

I was raised to obey. To obey my parents, to obey my duties as a woman, and to obey God were all lashed into me from the day I was born. No amount of leniency was ever given to me or any of the children for that matter. They took pleasure in our sorrow; it gave them a sense of power. And if I ever spoke my mind on the subject, my mother or father would strike me. I can't recall how many numerous occasions it happened. I simply know that I was the victim of their abuse more than anyone else.

Over time, I grew sick of the beatings and busied myself with the quietude of the forest. The trees hid me from their sight. The forest quickly became my friend, my soul. I learned much from it each day. The trees would speak to me and guide my every being, showing me their superior way of living. I spent so much time away from the others that they often sent search parties after me. But the trees concealed me every time, and eventually, the search parties stopped searching. My family and everyone else gave up on trying to fix me. Instead, each time I returned home, I would receive the highest degree of punishment that a child could be given. My body would become bound with scars and bruises. The once young and beautiful face that I was given from birth was no longer recognizable; I had the expression of a war-torn soldier at the age of 13. They would question what I was doing in the woods for such long periods of time and all I could tell them was, "Learning." And it was the truth. But those diseased creatures would only scowl and continue to hit me. I *was* innocent.

There was an exact day when I reached my breaking point, an exact moment I realized I would no longer accept the abuse, an exact second I felt the rage stop ticking.

We had been on the brink of starvation for some time, yet nobody had the courage to do anything about it. The men refused to act like men. They were cowards and they let us suffer. So, when my mother ordered me to fix up supper one night, I disobeyed. All I did was shake my head no, and I saw my mother's hand raise into the air. Before she had the chance to strike me, I shoved her backward. I assumed that as thin as I was, no amount of force I used would do very much. But I was wrong. My mother stumbled back until she hit the dinner table. A knife on the table fell to the floor along with my mother. The blade dropped at such a perfect angle that it went right through her hand. I froze momentarily, a smirk spreading across my face. She saw my expression and released a blood-curdling scream. That woman played the victim too well for anyone to believe it was an accident. I knew the punishment for this would be far worse than anything I had previously experienced, so I ran.

I took cover in the forest for some time. I knew the trees would protect the sole fact of my innocence. Yet, the more I thought about it, the more I wished I *had* shoved the knife through my mother's hand. It would have been far more satisfying to see the undeniable fear in her eyes when I spilled her blood with my own hands – a fair exchange for the years of abuse I suffered.

Not too long after the incident, the people of my meager community began to search for me, except this time it wasn't for my well-being. That night, they scoured the land, heaving their torches furiously into the air. There were moments when the eyes of a man nearly fell upon me, but something blinded him, a higher power. And no, I do not speak of God. He never protected me from them before, there would be no reason for Him to do it now. I speak of the Dark One. God's opposite. He concealed me in my time of need and blinded the eyes of vicious men with no good intent in their hearts. I observed these foul beings with nothing other than disgust. They accused me of evil and yet they were the ones who dared to act on cruelty towards a child.

The sun rose and the men had gone. My dreary eyes saw the golden rays peek through the trees. I came out of hiding and listened to the whispers of the forest. A voice was calling out to me. Its pleasant tone gave me a sense of security – something I hadn't felt in a long time. It circled around me in the breeze, whispering the most wonderful promises. I shut my eyes and listened to every word incandescently. The voice brought me to my knees, allowing me to feel all the energy that flowed through the earth. It was powerful, but it was dark. I absorbed this energy willingly, seeking all the sweet promises that were bestowed upon my soul, and giving in to the darkness. From then on, I served one master in exchange for extraordinary gifts that could far surpass the human capability, gifts that would bring me justice.

I used my newfound powers to avenge the pure version of my soul that was now gone from existence. In the night, when the hateful fools were tucked away in their beds, I rested my hand against the bark of a young maple tree that sat on the edge of the forest. I set a seed of poison within it that quickly spread down to the tree's roots and into the ground. It crawled along the soil like a cluster of spiders, untameable. The darkness made every single plant and crop and seedling crumble to dust. The wildflowers in the fields wilted until they were completely drained of all their vitality. I guaranteed that everything in my path would fade. If anything, I was doing those people a favor.

They were already bound to die of starvation, I only sped up the process.

~ 13 ~

TUCKER

This time, I was extra early when I arrived at the haunted house. There were no mysterious hold-ups or accidents that tried to stop me along my path.

As I got to the parking lot, I noticed a very gaunt figure standing by the entrance. It was Anthony, looking as deranged as ever. I smiled at him as I rode by, just trying to be friendly, but he actually spoke to me this time in coherent sentences.

"Mr. Romero," he said with a feeble voice.

I stopped and planted my foot on the ground. I had no idea what sort of insanity of his I was going to have to deal with, and frankly, I would've preferred to never have spoken to him again.

"What's up, Anthony?" I replied.

The man was physically shaking. He clasped his hands together awkwardly as if trying to steady himself. He no longer looked me in the eye with his usual crazy stare, but instead, he gazed at the dirt.

"Are you okay?" I asked sincerely. As much as I didn't like the man, I knew he needed help.

Anthony glanced up at me with tears forming in his eyes. "I'm trapped," his voice shook. The tears began to stream down his face. "You're trapped. We fell for her plan. We're dead men," he wailed. He threw his arms around me pitifully and wept. His pained cries could be heard throughout the entire property.

"Shh, shh," I hushed him anxiously. I held onto the man's arms in an effort to keep him from collapsing. "It's alright," I said, my eyes darting around to see if Shiloh was watching.

"No, no, no," he continued. His vocal cords sounded old and worn out as if he had aged about 30 years.

Just then, Shiloh appeared out of thin air. "Gentleman," she called out from behind us.

We both turned in terror. The woman stood perfectly still with her hands hidden behind her back. Her gaze fell on Anthony, and it was brutal. I looked down at Anthony who appeared to be struggling to even breathe. All of a sudden, I got flashbacks to the previous time something like this had happened.

"Hey, hey," I said, trying to lift him to his feet.

"Anthony," Shiloh spoke ominously, almost in a taunting manner. Her red lips formed a fierce scowl.

The man kept his head aimed toward the ground as he shook uncontrollably.

"Stand," she hissed.

"I think there's something wrong," I told her with a worried expression, still trying to hold him upright.

"Oh, I'm sure there is. Anthony, stand. Now," Shiloh said coldly.

I couldn't understand why she was so heartless. I knew that was her usual personality, but it was clear the man needed some sort of medical attention.

Anthony gripped my arms and began to lift himself with all his strength. Shiloh watched relentlessly, refusing to step in and help him. For a moment, Anthony looked at me intensely. He began to mouth words almost silently to me. "The. Devil. Is. Here." My eyes widened as he switched his gaze to Shiloh. Luckily, she didn't seem to hear or see what he had said.

"Good," Shiloh said as Anthony finally let go of my arms.

The man stumbled back and stood up as straight as possible. He kept his arms flatly pinned to his sides like a soldier. Even with all that I had witnessed, this was easily one of the strangest things to encounter.

"Anthony, would you please clean up the barn?" Shiloh muttered, narrowing her eyes at him.

"B-but," he stuttered.

"Now," she ordered. Shiloh always had the last word. Nobody could handle the tension of her gaze, let alone her rigid voice. Plus, just based on his behavior, I had a feeling that Anthony received a stronger form of punishment for any slight disrespect towards Shiloh.

Anthony scurried past us, repeating the phrase, "I'm sorry, I'm so sorry."

Once he was gone, Shiloh turned to me sharply. "What did he tell you?" she interrogated, squinting her eyes. The pitch-black eyeliner only made her green eyes even more intense. It was alarming and magnetic all at the same time.

"Nothing," I answered. I could feel my heart rate increasing as she stared me down. "Just his usual crazy talk," I added quickly.

I could feel my heart thumping in my chest, and it was almost as if Shiloh could feel it too. She looked me up and down with those emerald eyes. It was clear she was trying to break me down until I spilled the truth. We maintained eye contact for what felt like forever until she finally looked away.

"Alright then," she said casually. "There isn't too much prep work for us to do tonight. So, just sit in the greenhouse until I call you out."

I nodded and immediately made my way over to the greenhouse. There was no way I was about to show her any signs of disrespect after what just happened.

I waited in the structure for at least an hour, fidgeting anxiously and observing the odd spectacles that surrounded me. When Shiloh finally entered the greenhouse, she had an unhappy expression on her face, and I mean more than usual. I was wary to speak to her at all, let alone ask if something was wrong, so I decided to keep my mouth shut.

"Are you ready?" Shiloh asked, handing me the serpent necklace once again.

"Yes," I mumbled, nervously placing the leather cord over my head. I tried to avoid looking her in the eye, yet I could feel her gaze on me at all times. I could tell she was still caught up in the encounter with Anthony. She was perfectly aware that I knew something she didn't want me to know.

I was about to leave the greenhouse when Shiloh said my name. I faced the door and kept my hand on the handle as she spoke.

"Tucker, remember, do not enter the forest. You are simply there to aid the customers."

I nodded and rushed outside. As much as I wanted her to trust me, I wasn't doing a very good job. In fact, I was only making things worse for myself.

I spent the night shivering from a combination of cold air and fear. There were no specifically terrifying encounters like the previous night, but I caught multiple glimpses of glowing eyes with faint silhouettes traveling through the trees. Although there was limited vision, there appeared to be beings of all shapes and sizes, but still, none of them were human.

When the night was over, I hurried back to the front entrance with my hands tucked deep in my pockets. Even the giant security jacket was no match for the frigid outdoor temperature. I often questioned how the leaves were still on any of the trees with how cold it got, but then again, that forest was magical.

I was apprehensive to see Shiloh again, but to my surprise, she was in a far better mood. She sauntered up to me with a very slight grin; it was about the most I had ever seen her smile. I could just barely see the flawlessly white teeth behind her lips. They were all lined up in an exact formation. This woman's outward appearance seemed perfect, and yet, I knew that was the farthest thing from true.

"Another *wonderful* night," she announced, looking down at me.

I gave her a tired smile, hoping she'd keep the conversation to a minimum and therefore keep her suspicions to a minimum as well.

"I hope you didn't experience any troubles," Shiloh added.

"Nope."

"Good. Then, I will see you back here next Friday. No need to come in during the week," she said. There was so much distrust in her eyes as if she thought I wasn't going to come back. I waited a moment before responding, allowing her to dissect every bit of my soul.

"I'll be there," I finally told her.

That night, when I went home, I tried to remove the haunted house from my mind completely. I wanted so badly to be wrong about it, but that itching feeling always came back. God was telling me to wake up and pay attention, and if I didn't do it soon enough, it could be too late.

I knew Asher and Charli would be mad at me for not investigating better, but it wasn't really my fault. I was dealing with someone or *something* far more powerful than any of us.

I entered my darkened house, carrying all my equipment and a slim stack of money from the night. The floorboards creaked under my shoes and each time it caused me to flinch. I tried to move quickly, while also not waking my parents. But with my luck, I ran right into a kitchen chair. It let out a loud squeak on the wooden floor and my head shot up. A low grumble sounded from my parents' room. That's when I booked it. No longer caring about making noise, I ran to my room as fast as I could, nearly dropping the money as I went. When I heard the final click of my door locking behind me, I let out a relieved sigh. I was safe. My parents were too lazy to try and break my door down in the middle of the night.

I fell into a deep sleep at some point and awoke to an empty house. I can't tell you how thrilled I was. My morning was peaceful for once; there wouldn't be any screaming or opportunities for me to get another black eye. I made myself breakfast and turned on the TV for some background noise. Yes, I know, I just explained how it was peaceful and quiet for once, but I needed some sort of background noise. I guess I had grown so used to the constant sounds that the thought of utter silence in that house made me uncomfortable.

Doing a happy little dance around the kitchen table with a bowl of cereal in hand, I noticed the news station was back on. Almost coincidentally, there was another missing person case. This time, it was a teenage boy, and of course, his last known destination was Soul of the Wilderness. They wouldn't release the exact details of the boy's death, instead, they just said his mangled body had been found on the edge of a forest near a gas station.

Despite that strange part of me that wanted to defend Shiloh, I knew I couldn't. There were only so many coincidences that could be believed.

I wasted no time in getting to Asher's house. Cars

honked at me as I sped past them on my bike. At one point I was pedaling so fast that I thought the tires might just fly off.

When I got to his front door, I was met with a pleasant smile from his mother. She looked at my sweat-ridden face with curiosity.

"Tucker? Is everything alright?" she asked in that sweet motherly tone that she seemed to permanently have.

I always loved getting to talk to Asher's parents, and Charli's too. They had been so kind from the day I met them. The truth is, these complete strangers made me feel more loved than my own parents ever had. Their love made me forget about the cruelty I would have to return to.

"Hi, Mrs. Castillo," I fought to catch my breath, "Is Asher here? I need to talk to him about something kinda important."

"Oh, of course. Come in," she said happily, opening the door wider.

My eyes wandered the house as Mrs. Castillo called for Asher. Their house was so clean and decorative compared to mine. It actually felt like a home.

Just then, Asher appeared from the kitchen. His hands and knees were coated in dirt.

"Hey," he grinned, "Sorry, I was helping my dad with some stuff outside and I-" his smile faded as he looked more closely at me.

"Asher."

"What's wrong?" he furrowed his brow.

"It's about Ms. Farrington."

~ 14 ~

METSAH

For days, I walked amongst the trees. My master gave me what I needed and I was *prospering*. I watched the humans from afar as their suffering kicked in. They could no longer even muster a smile under those unbearable conditions I had so readily created for them. No man or woman could amount to the freedom of my being.

After taking the time necessary to regain my strength in concealment, I went out from the woods. The moment I set a single toe on their land, the people turned their heads to me in amazement. They could feel the vibration of dark energy I carried with me. I saw the terrified faces of mothers dragging their children back into their pathetic little cottages. Even the men refused to approach, grasping their shovels and pitchforks as if those were going to save them. It became apparent that not one of them recognized my now healthy presentation. The skin on my face was glowing full and radiantly – something they could never attain. I stepped through their rows of death and despair, admiring my work. Every plant that was once an opportunity to feed their starving children was crunching weakly under my feet.

"Who are you?" a male voice cried out. He put on the persona of a bear, but he was not a bear.

I gazed at this man. His beard was shriveling, as was his skin that sunk deeply into his face. When I looked at him, all I saw was a frightened little cub. This man, and all the others, were now the unrecognizable ones. Their vulnerability made me laugh.

"Who are you?" the man repeated more violently. Then, he neared and I knew I was looking at my father. His lower lip quivered once he finally perceived me correctly as his child. "Metsah," he mumbled.

My gaze narrowed at the utterance of my name. "You've grown weak, Father," my tongue scorned. Out of the corner of my eye, I noticed the fearful gaze of my mother hiding within the tiny cottage I used to live in.

The true weakness of my father began to peek through. Tears were forming in his eyes. "Y-you did this to us. You killed everything," he wept, sounding almost uncertain of his claims.

I allowed him to see my satisfied grin.

The man let out feeble whimpers, expressing his anguish. I believe it was at that moment that he saw a flash of the Devil in my eyes. His sorrow slowly turned to wrath. "What is this evil you have conjured? What curse have you brought upon us?" he cried furiously, spit emanating from his mouth.

"I chose my freedom."

His expression became repulsed. "That's what you think this is? You've damned us all!" A vein emerged from his bright red forehead.

I leaned closer. "No, Father. You did that to yourselves." My eyes met with his and I could suddenly smell the fear that resonated in his soul. "I'm simply putting my resources to good use. Perhaps it's something you should have done a long time ago. It may have saved us," I hissed.

"How dare you speak such blasphemy. You have betrayed God," my father retorted.

"I?" I couldn't help but chuckle. "Well, I think He would be rather disappointed in all of you as well." I looked around at all of their paltry faces. The remnants of shame were evident in their eyes. "All of you look at me with such disgust," I paused, absorbing their guilt, "And yet you are no better. Your God hates you just as much as He hates me!"

The man could not utter a word, he simply looked on in astonishment. I gazed upon his frailty. I knew it would be so easy to strike him down as he once did unto me.

"Are you prepared to meet Him?" I spoke sharply.

The resentment in my father's eyes was precise.

"Yes, the one who let us suffer. The one who taught obedience through cruelty. The one who cannot and *will not* save you now." I tightened my jaw with each word. "Or perhaps you won't meet Him at all. No," I grinned, "Instead you'll get the undeserved opportunity to meet my Creator . . . the *better* Creator."

The man shook his head slightly, taking a step back.

"Master," I whispered, calling to be replenished with

power. An electricity traveled through the ground and into my hands. I could feel it building within. I watched storm clouds gather in the sky, believing it was my master gathering what I needed . . . but I was deceived. In the blink of an eye, the electricity within my bones suddenly vanished, as did the rest of my strength. My knees dropped to the dirt. I placed my hands on the ground, attempting to stand back up, but I could not. It felt as though an invisible force was holding me down.

A few moments later, I felt multiple pairs of hands wrap around my arms. They lifted me and I could see the faces of people circling me. My legs and lungs worked vigorously as I kicked and screamed, but it was no use. All of my power had left me. My master had abandoned me.

The mob of people dragged me deep into the forest until they came upon the poisoned tree. Its mutated black bark and wretched scent made them gag in disgust. Two men held me forcibly against the tree as a rope was tightened around my torso. Once the rope was bound, everyone stepped back to see the shame on my face. I struggled to the best of my ability, but I was unable to break free.

"You have turned your back on God, Metsah," one of the men stated.

"He turned His back on *me!*" I screamed through gritted teeth. My dark hair flew around chaotically as a breeze flowed through the trees. The wind carried my fury, but it also carried my grief. After all, I was only a child.

Whispers sounded from among the crowd of judgmental faces. They were no better than I. They deserved the same trial I was about to receive.

"You have allowed the Devil into your soul. You are a witch," the man announced for all of them to hear.

I couldn't physically accept his words; they made my skin itch with rage. I mumbled hushed whispers as the man spoke, ignoring his blatant ignorance.

"Therefore," he peered down at me, "You must burn with the Devil." His eyes held no sympathy, not one drop. He hated me, and so did the rest of them.

I watched in horror as one of the men lit a torch. My body fought more than ever to escape from that wretched snare. I strained so much that the rope began to cut right through my fair skin. The whispers from my tongue grew more rapid in pace, refusing to stop.

The flame approached, carrying the fury of God within it. It looked me dead in the eyes, threatening a pain soon to be.

The man knelt down next to me, taunting me with the fire. He waved it near my face, allowing the burning sensation to preview. He looked at me with such a smug glare. It was infuriating. He was so busy taunting me that he didn't see me blow on the flames. They struck his face like a thousand blades and he fell back. He kept a hand over his eye as he cried in pain. As multiple people went to his aid, my father, out of everyone there, was the one to lift the torch from the ground and carry it back over to me.

"You evil little child," he murmured. His voice was pure hatred. "You're going to burn for eternity."

I smirked at him. The Devil had returned to me. "*And you'll all burn with me,*" we hissed.

In the blink of an eye, my entire body was engulfed

in flames. I kept quiet and let them eat away at my skin until there was nothing left. My soul was bound to the darkness, but it was pledged to return.

~ 15 ~

TUCKER

Before we discussed anything, Asher and I made sure Charli was with us. The second we told her what it was about, she sprinted down the street to Asher's house. As ridiculing as she was, we needed her help. Charli always found holes in stories that no one else ever did.

I told them everything I knew and everything I could remember in great detail. We went back and forth over pieces of the story for hours until it was completely comprehended.

Eventually, Asher fell silent. He intertwined his fingers and tapped his jaw, looking endlessly into the wall. I stared at him from the floor, waiting for him to lecture me again on my poor decisions.

"So?" I raised my eyebrows at him. "What do I do?"

Asher began to shake his head. "Tuck . . . looks like we're going on a witch hunt," he said casually, laying his hands in his lap.

"We don't know if she's actually a witch," I rolled my eyes.

"No? Then what else would you call her? She sounds like a reincarnation of some 1800s witch if you ask me," Charli jeered. "But you know, like an actual one."

"Look, I'm pretty sure we could dig up some information about her and that place. There's gotta be an old news article online or something," Asher spoke up. He sprung from his seat and opened the laptop on his desk. He got to typing with zero hesitation.

My heart raced with that same guilty feeling as I watched him search through the various articles that popped up. I shut my eyes for a moment and shoved that stupid feeling as far down as possible.

Just then, Asher yelled, "Bingo!"

I leaped up from my seat on the ground and ran to his side. "What'd you find?"

"Take a look," he pointed at the screen, "Her family's name made headlines."

The title of the article read: **"Farrington Family Business in Hot Water After Mysterious Death."**

"Apparently the 'death' was her mother," Asher explained. His eyes twitched frantically as he scrolled through. "Oh. It says she got poisoned. But the funny thing is, it doesn't sound like anyone ever questioned Shiloh," he added, giving me a funny glance.

"You really think she would've poisoned her own mother? Shiloh was just a little kid at the time," I said with a scowl. At first, I couldn't even come up with a reason for why or how a child could do something like that, but then, I remembered my own situation. My eyes wandered the room in a haunting manner. "Maybe the mother was the evil one. Maybe Shiloh wanted to escape *her*."

Asher and Charli didn't say anything. Then again, they didn't have to. I knew they didn't want to make things more uncomfortable by giving their own thoughts on the subject since they didn't share the same experiences as I did growing up.

"Didn't you say that the bar owner next door to the haunted house was on the news?" Charli brought up suddenly. "What if we go talk to him?"

"You think he'll be open to talking to three random kids?" I asked.

The two of them gave me the same irked expression.

"Are you kidding?" Charli giggled almost sarcastically. She tilted her head to the side with a goofy smirk. "The man will get to complain about the one person he seems to hate most in the world. He's probably dying to talk to someone who actually believes his side of the story."

Asher nodded in agreeance.

"Well then I guess we better get going," I sighed.

The three of us, not knowing what to expect, rode down to the bar on our bikes. Riding through Asher's neighborhood was the one positive thing about this whole experience. I got to look at all the nicely decorated homes that were lit up with pumpkins and autumn welcome signs on their porches. Oftentimes, we would see little kids running through the yards and pointing in amazement, trying to decide which house was the best. They couldn't wait to get dressed up in their costumes and see what all those award-winning houses looked like on Halloween night. I had only ever wished for a childhood like that.

As we approached the bar, I caught a glimpse of the haunted house and I felt my anxiety skyrocket. I didn't even realize how far ahead my friends were as I became entranced by the trees on the far side of the property. The woods were calling me back. The brushing of the leaves against one another sounded like a name. My name. "Tucker," voices whispered. They repeated my name over and over again. The tone of the voices were desperate and pained as if I had abandoned them for quite some time.

Suddenly, one very loud voice called my name. "Tucker!" It was Charli. Her and Asher were staring back at me from the front of the bar. "Tucker, let's go! Hurry up, slowpoke!" she shouted at me.

I forced my eyes away and sped past the haunted attraction.

"Are you good?" Asher asked me curiously as I rested my bike against the wall of the building.

"What? Oh, yeah," I nodded, trying to ignore his curiosities.

He gave me a sideways glance, clearly not convinced. That was his way of guilt-tripping me into saying more. He knew it usually worked too.

Luckily, Charli came to my rescue without even realizing it. "Come on," she said to us, waltzing right into the bar.

As I was about to follow her in, Asher grabbed my arm. "Tuck, what's that woman doing to your head?" he said in a low tone.

I didn't have a response at first. His serious manner surprised me. "Nothing," I finally answered. "Can we just get this done?" I brushed past him, avoiding any other confrontation.

The reaction from the people in the bar was just as you'd expect. They all turned their heads in unison with the same baffled look that said, "What the hell are three ragamuffin-looking children doing in a bar on a Sunday afternoon?"

We shuffled through the crowd awkwardly, well, except for Charli. Her confidence was unmatched anywhere we went. If she were wearing some different clothes, Charli might've fit right in with the rest of them. She sauntered past the jealous glares of women and their oddly-intrigued husbands, and placed her elbows casually on the bar.

Asher and I looked at each other briefly, knowing we had to go along with Charli's confident behavior if we wanted to get any information.

Just then, one of the bartenders began to talk to Charli. He had darker skin, like Asher and I, and his hair was beginning to gray from his sideburns down to his unshaven face. He had a beer gut that was even more pronounced under his stained white t-shirt. His expression was lined with bitterness as he observed young Charli standing so dauntlessly in front of his other customers. Their conversation was audible throughout almost the entire building because everyone was focused on our presence.

"Hi," Charli smirked, "We need to talk to the owner."

The man furrowed his brow as he filled more glasses at

the tap. "Now, what the hell could three kids need to talk to a bar owner about?" he asked boorishly.

"It's kind of private," Charli said quietly, doing her best to remain polite despite the man's tone.

"Uh-huh," he rolled his eyes, starting to walk to the opposite side of the bar, uninterested.

Charli glanced back at us nervously as if begging for help. But before Asher or I could even get a word in, she blurted out, "It's about the Farringtons."

If there was anyone left who hadn't been staring at us before, they definitely were now.

"Crap," Asher muttered under his breath as every pair of eyes watched us intensely.

The man made his way back over to us slowly. He signaled for the other bartender to take over for him. "Who are you?" he frowned at us, leaning uncomfortably close.

"I'm Charli. Tucker and Asher," she tilted her head towards us. "Listen, we just need to talk to the owner. Please," she pleaded.

The man scowled silently.

The tension in the whole building made it feel like we were about to get into one of those old Western bar fights from the movies.

"I am the owner," the man finally said. His brutish expression lightened as he held out a hand. "Russel Morales," he added as Charli shook his hand.

Finally, the chatter from everyone else started back up again. I felt a sense of relief run through my shoulders.

"So you wanna know about the Farringtons, huh? I

suppose you're not too fond of that family either then," Russel stated bluntly.

"Why do you say that?" Charli questioned.

"Everyone who comes to my bar shares the same opinion. They all know she's a murderous bitch. They just wanna see her for themselves. Typically you'd expect a murderer to look a bit distraught or unkempt. But this woman . . . she is certainly put together. I know it's just a cover-up, a disguise."

The noise got increasingly louder with chatter that I could only assume was about us. Every once in a while I would catch a short glimpse of someone peeking over at us suspiciously from their table.

"Is there any way we could talk to you outside? It's kind of difficult to hear in this place," Asher spoke up, giving the man an obviously uncomfortable stare.

Russel shook his head as he cleaned a glass. "No can do, kiddo. Her little spies might hear us out there," he said.

The three of us looked at each other in confusion.

"I'm sorry, but did you say 'spies?'" Charli asked.

"Yeah," he chuckled, "Those things are everywhere. I can't even get in my car without one of them watching me."

Our confusion only grew more and it was openly expressed on each of our faces.

"You know," his tone changed again, "The demonic pets she makes on that property. All of them live in that forest of hers. I constantly see their eyes poking out from the trees," Russel added. He talked about it like it was normal, but really he had just grown used to it.

I could feel Asher looking at me again. His eyes were practically burning into the side of my head. I knew he wanted me to say something about my own experience, but I couldn't muster up the courage to do it.

"Have you actually seen Shiloh kill anyone though?" Charli interrogated. I guess the talk of magical creatures in the woods finally brought out her skeptical side.

"I don't have to see it. I know it. She uses those beasts to kill people. If you go in there, there's a pretty solid chance you won't come back out, at least not alive. My niece and a couple of her friends visited that hellhole a few years ago. One of her friends went missing in there and they never found the poor kid. The people who show up dead on the side of the road are the lucky ones."

The three of us sat in silence for a moment, not knowing what to say next.

Then, the man began to chuckle. "Even the previous owner knew something was up with that place. If it wasn't Shiloh who cursed it, someone else definitely did."

"Who was the previous owner?" Asher asked.

"An old guy named Cliff Ross." Russell held up a hand, "Don't bother looking him up on those phones of yours. The man was old when he had the place. He's more than dead by now," he continued to chuckle softly.

Charli looked at him with a furrowed brow. "Do you know if he has any relatives nearby?"

"Now why would I know a thing like that? You'll have to do that digging on your own, kid," the man said gruffly.

Then, I exchanged an odd glance with Russel; it was one of the first times I had made eye contact with him during that whole interaction. He looked me up and down suspiciously. I pulled my eyes away and looked around the rest of the bar, trying not to get myself involved in any sort of unwanted conversation with him.

"What's up with you, kid?" Russel asked.

I knew his question was directed at me. I could still feel his eyes on me before I even turned back to look at him. He squinted as if he saw something in me that he didn't like.

It felt like my voice had completely left me. I couldn't find a single word for a response.

Asher and Charli began to look at me oddly as well, thinking I had done or said something they weren't aware of.

"He just doesn't like talking to strangers a whole lot," Charli said in my defense.

"Huh," the man huffed. "Well, you came into my bar looking for answers."

I shifted uncomfortably.

"Actually, Tucker has some stories about Shiloh too," Asher announced, "Right, Tuck?" He looked at me eagerly, pushing me to spill the information.

I don't think I had ever been so annoyed with him in my life. Subtly, I shook my head at Asher, desperate for him to shut up.

"What do you mean? Have you visited the place or somethin'?" Russell interrogated, looking between the two of us.

Asher ignored my plea and continued on. "He just started working there actually."

I bit down on the insides of my cheeks, trying to control the chaos of emotions that were running through my head and stomach. For someone as quiet as I was around strangers, there was no worse feeling than being pushed to talk when you have nothing to say.

Russel's eye grew wide and an agape frown formed on his face. "You work there? And you thought it was a good idea to come *here*?" he exclaimed irately. He slammed the glass in his hand onto the tabletop, catching the attention of all the customers again.

To say the least, we were all shocked by his strange outburst. I immediately felt my shoulders closing in.

"No, no, no," Russel heaved, "You can't be in here. She's already gotten to you. I'm not going to have her dark magic infect my business. You need to leave right now." He began waving his hands all around as if to shoo us out. "Go! Now!" he yelled, his face turning a dark shade of red.

"Okay, okay. We're going. Sorry to trouble you," Charli said, shoving Asher and I forcibly toward the doors.

The three of us fumbled past people in a frantic manner. Everyone glared as if we had done something wrong. Some even scooted their chairs away as we passed by like we had a contagious disease. Any fear I had of stage-fright was certainly coming back to my mind. Actually, this was far past stage-fright; this was just public embarrassment.

As we got outside, Charli let out a loud huff. "What was that about? Does he really think something's attached to you?"

Asher glanced at me worryingly. "What if you do?"

I glared at him. Asher was already progressively getting

on my nerves and now he wanted to accuse me of something he hadn't fully understood. "What?" I responded with exasperation.

"I mean, what if Shiloh put some sort of attachment on you? Are you really going to deny that it's a possibility? Tucker, you have not been acting normal since you started working there. I swear it's like she is getting in your head somehow and you just won't tell us," Asher explained.

I didn't want to accept that something was possibly wrong with me, but Asher had a good point.

"Is she talking to you in your head? Are you seeing visions or something?" Charli chimed in.

My brain started to feel overloaded. I couldn't get a solid thought out. And their constant berating wasn't helping. I squeezed my eyes shut and tried to focus, but they continued with more questions.

"No! No! I don't know!" I shouted suddenly.

They immediately stopped and gave me a fearful look.

I sighed. "I don't know," I spoke quieter. My voice was so weak. "It's like that place has some sort of hold on me. Like if I expose it then I get punished. I can't describe it."

Asher placed a comforting hand on my shoulder. "We're not gonna let this thing get to you, but you *have to* expose it. People need to know the truth or else she's just going to keep killing them off. You've got to help us out here, Tuck."

"And God's not going to let anything bad happen to you. You're helping the good side, remember?" Charli asserted.

I nodded hesitantly. "The good side," I repeated quietly.

As the words left my mouth, I felt a spark of hope hit my chest.

~ 16 ~

METSAH

My fury had grown far past any amount of control with Anthony. He had sworn himself to work under my command in return for his own survival. The pathetic creature was barely holding on to his last vestige; the final pieces of life were slipping from his very sight when I found him. His soul was suffering as so many do when they are abandoned by their God. So I gave him a new God to serve, a better God. And yet, as all humans do, the young man revealed his ungrateful nature. He betrayed me, but more importantly, he betrayed the darkness. Once you leave, you cannot return, not by choice. We will simply drag you back and there will be nothing but agony to endure.

When the young boy, Tucker, had finally gone, I summoned Anthony back to my presence. His fear was constant and unbreaking. He knew he had done wrong by me. He continuously begged for mercy, but the man had forgotten that the Devil is not forgiving, not in the slightest.

I brought him to the edge of the woods so that my

children could smell his despair. They cackled and hooted, growing impatient for their dinner.

"Please! I'm sorry, Shiloh! I am begging you for forgiveness. Please!" Anthony cried. Shameful tears rolled down his cheeks, dying once they hit the unholy ground.

"You know my name, Anthony. Go ahead," I hissed, "Say it."

He couldn't even muster the courage to follow such orders.

"What's wrong? You were so willing to tell that boy who I was from the start. Weren't you? You took every opportunity you had to speak with him. And did you not also try to give him subtle hints with your demonic drawings?" I let my acrimony resonate in my tone.

"I-I d-didn't want him t-to get hurt."

"Oh, of course not, dear. But that isn't your decision, is it?" I bent down slightly to meet his gaze.

His watering eyes wouldn't go anywhere in my direction. Instead, they twitched uncontrollably, the blood vessels growing more and more red by the second.

"You abandoned your precious duty and have thus proven yourself disloyal. And you know what I must do," I told him.

His entire body shook with each word. He cowered beneath me like a frightened little mouse, his whiskers trembling. "P-please, Metsah," Anthony finally voiced. "I've served you well."

A pleased grin struck the edges of my mouth. "Yes, you have," I gently stroked his hair. It was so amusing to see that tiny spark of hope in his eyes for just a moment. And it was even more amusing to watch it fade. I took a force-ful hold of his hair. "And now you will serve my children just as well. They're quite hungry."

The man crumbled to the ground in mental agony, un-able to accept the consequences. His eyes traveled along the trees as my children stalked just beyond. "No," he quivered.

"Your soul is so tormented, Anthony. It's filled with all the nourishment my loves need in order to live. They will feast upon it with great pleasure, I'm sure."

My creatures grew more boisterous by the second. The overwhelming scent of the man's vitality wasting away was driving them mad.

"Keres," I called adamantly, "Take him."

~ 17 ~

TUCKER

Asher, Charli, and I carried our secret with unrest as we walked alongside the other kids in our school. It was crazy to think that none of them had any idea what we had gotten ourselves into just over the past couple of weeks.

That day, we had been discussing how I was going to sneak into the haunt after school and try to dig up some more information, or at least an ounce of proof. The two of them were obviously excited but at the same time very worried for my safety.

"You need to find a way to get into that barn. I'm sure she's got some sort of horrific thing in there that helps her make those creatures so realistic," Charli told me in a quiet voice, trying not to draw the attention of everyone around us.

Asher peered at her with a furrowed brow. "What do you mean? What 'horrific' thing would she possibly have?"

I glanced at Asher with a slight chuckle as we prepared ourselves for the oddity of Charli's brain.

"I don't know. Maybe she uses like dead animals or something. How else could she have made that werewolf thing that Tucker saw?" Charli blurted out.

"Or, you know, there's this thing called fake fur," Asher teased.

Being stuck in the middle, I scrunched my shoulders, ready for the fighting to ensue. They glared at each other from opposite sides. Sometimes it was amusing to watch them argue, except when one of them was ready to physically attack the other. Usually, it was Charli who did that.

"Oh wow, thank you for your wonderful insight, Asher. But next time, keep it to yourself," Charli sneered.

Asher gave her a contemptuous smirk. "Sorry, I just thought your pitifully slow brain cells might need some help catching up."

"You know what-"

And there went that fist of Charli's. I could see her clenching every finger out of the corner of my eye. If she hit him, Asher would be more than ready to hit back, just like every sibling pair in the world. But in their case, Charli would likely win, despite how strong Asher might've been. Her level of lunacy would outweigh his muscles any day.

"Anyways!" I stated abruptly, raising my hands in front of them to prevent any punches from being thrown. "I'm going to sneak in later and try not to get caught. Then, I'll let you guys know what I find."

They both let out grumpy sighs.

"And what if you *do* get caught?" Charli asked, returning to her normal tone.

I shrugged. "I don't know. I guess I'll just have to make something up on the spot. But for now, let's pray that doesn't happen," I said, getting that phantom nervous feeling in the pit of my stomach.

For the rest of our time together, we walked mostly in silence. We were all going over the situation again and again in our heads, questioning how it was even real.

As we cut through the grass out front, fallen leaves crunched under our shoes. I peered down at all the different shades, and as I did, I could almost imagine faces in each one of them. One large, blood-red leaf got caught on the front of my shoe momentarily and I was reminded of those werewolf eyes. The leaf quickly blew past me, but the recurring image of those eyes did not.

"Well," Asher sighed as we approached our bikes, "Good luck, soldier."

He and Charli both saluted in a comical manner as I got onto my bike. I did the same back to them and headed towards the place that frightened me the most on this Earth.

I left my bike a little ways down the road so that Shiloh wouldn't be able to see it. Then, I snuck onto the property from behind the barn. My clumsy body managed to take a tumble while climbing over the short, three-foot-tall fence that sat on the perimeter. Fortunately, I remained completely unseen.

I crept along the side of the barn, expecting that I would have to use the main sliding doors at the front which were huge and noisy, but then, I discovered a regular-sized door on the side. It had all sorts of old, rusty tools and equipment strewn about at its entrance as if to keep people from ever using it. I carefully maneuvered myself through without making a peep. As I placed my hand on the rickety door knob, I felt a pounding heartbeat in my temple. I was probably one of the worst intruders of all time. With one last check behind me, I slowly twisted the handle. Thankfully, it wasn't locked, but it didn't exactly open easily. It seemed like there was something blocking the door on the other side, or the hinges were just cemented in place after not being used for so long. Placing my shoulder against the door, I gave a gentle push. The door squeaked open with resistance, revealing a screen of complete darkness. Using the light from my phone, I carefully stepped inside onto the concrete floor.

For a brief moment, everything was totally silent. I didn't know whether to be calm or frightened by the quietness. Just then, the squeaking of the door started back up and it slammed shut behind me. I jolted forward and nearly dropped my only source of light. Now, my nerves were definitely on edge. I aimed my phone towards the door to check one last time, but it appeared to just be me inside the barn. Oh boy, was I wrong.

When I turned back to the rest of the interior, my heart skipped a few beats. All the unfinished faces of Shiloh's latest projects were now visible. Their twisted frames created eerie shadows on the walls. Looking at all of them quickly reminded me why I hated the barn so much. There was one in particular that I really hated. It was located closest to the big barn doors at the very front of its row.

The unfinished creation had the torso of a human and arms that were almost completely done. Surprisingly, that wasn't what I hated about it. I hated the eight, elongated legs that it stood on. Usually, the sight of anything with eight legs only meant one thing: spiders. I hated spiders.

I wandered through the rows of creatures over and over again, hoping to find something a bit more unusual. I even searched the second story but all I found was an array of normal building materials. All the bins and containers were labeled, except for one. I was hesitant to go near it, but knowing my luck that would be the one container with actual evidence in it. Crouching down, I snapped the plastic locks off and lifted the lid. At first, I thought I was seeing a combination of human and animal hair piled together. Then, I realized it was just a bunch of fake fur and crappy wigs. I sat back on my heels and let out a sigh of relief. The recurring doubt struck me again. "What am I doing?" I mumbled to myself, looking around as I sat in a dark, decrepit barn that I didn't even have permission to be in.

Suddenly, my phone light was not the only light I saw in the darkness. A faint orange glow appeared from behind me. I spun around and looked down below, realizing that one of the props did have eyes . . . bright, orange eyes. I ducked down behind one of the boxes in a panic. I was positive that nobody else had entered the barn, and yet, somehow, those eyes were lit up.

I shuffled to the staircase, making sure to keep my phone off. As I made my way back down, I kept one eye on the steps and one eye on the orange light at all times.

Just as I reached the bottom step, one of my feet slipped and hit a piece of sheet metal on the ground. The annoyingly loud *clang* attracted the attention of not only myself but the eyes as well. I didn't know how, but those orange eyes shifted in my direction. Without a second thought, I sprinted towards the door. My clumsy feet ran into every possible object within a five-foot radius. I scrambled to reach the doorknob, nearly falling on my face in the process.

Once outside, I yanked the door shut and stupidly ran out into the open. It took a second before the realization hit my brain. It was only by the grace of God that Shiloh hadn't seen me run out of there in broad daylight.

I was more than ready to leave and get my bike, but a sudden overwhelming feeling popped into my head. My eyes traveled the property with deep curiosity. As much as I wanted to deny it, I knew, and everyone else knew, that something unusual was happening there.

I then looked at the greenhouse which stood less than a hundred feet away. The silhouette of a tall figure was visible through the plastic walls. It hadn't been there before, which meant it had to be another one of Shiloh's creations, but it also meant that it was close to finished.

This time, due to my own ignorance, I had forgotten to double-check if anyone was around. I made my way toward the greenhouse with determination written all over my face, but as I approached the door, Shiloh's voice sounded from behind me.

"Mr. Romero."

I stopped dead in my tracks. Just the cold sound of her

voice made me feel like I was committing an unspeakable crime. My brain raced to think of an excuse as I turned around to face her at the pace of a snail.

"Mr. Romero? What are you doing here?" Shiloh looked me up and down with those piercing green eyes.

"I think I left my wallet in the greenhouse," I replied quickly and without a single stutter. I was surprised by the level of confidence in my answer; perhaps it would throw her off my trail.

"Why didn't you ask me if I had found it?" she questioned.

Uh oh. My confidence was rapidly depleting. "Well, I uh-"

Her eyes were literally staring into my soul. Once again, I saw the pupils become snake-like slits. She tilted her head down slightly, narrowing her gaze.

"I didn't want to bother you. I figured I could just grab it quickly," I finally said. My hands were beginning to shake with nerves. I folded my arms and tucked my hands away, trying to stabilize myself before she noticed.

"I haven't seen a wallet. I was in there this morning." The suspicion on her face was increasingly evident.

"Oh," I chuckled nervously, "Really? Well, that sucks for me then. I guess I just didn't search my house well enough."

Shiloh definitely wasn't amused. Her expression was emotionless, but also full of anger. We stood across from each other in awkward silence. I felt like I was being cornered by a hungry lion. One wrong move and I'd get eaten alive.

"I think it's time for you to go, Mr. Romero. I'll see you again on Friday," Shiloh said. Her voice still carried every ounce of suspicion she had for me. And those eyes . . . they never broke contact.

I nodded nervously. Ripping my eyes away from hers, I rushed past her toward the parking lot.

I didn't look back until I finally got to my bike that lay halfway down the road. Although I could no longer see her, I felt as though her eyes were still watching me. All of their eyes were.

~ 18 ~

METSAH

It was for the final time that I put my faith in a human being. That young boy, Tucker, was a result of my own ignorance, my own sightless desperation to be served. His youthful naivety tricked both him and I. He had been so incredibly ill-judged during his initial arrival that his first impression of my true character was an utter lie. I took pity on the boy and I still do. I saw something in him that connected deeply to the little girl who had been abused for so long and burned at that damned tree. I hoped to bring Tucker to the realization that these cruel, insufferable people would never care for him. But I suppose, like the rest, he didn't see it the way I saw it. Although, as much as the boy was just like the others, he had something much different about him. He had his God. Truly.

Converting one to the darkness tends to be the simplest task in the world. Humans are so blinded by their greed and their vanity and their lust and most importantly, their *pride.* It is beyond rare that you ever find one who does not live for those things, and yet, there was Tucker. He lived for love. I knew breaking him down would be near impossible from the moment he stepped onto the property.

The day I discovered his knowledge of what I was and who I served, was the same day my last bit of humanity vanished. There remained the slight mercy in my heart that did not want any harm to come to the boy, but it could not be.

When Tucker left, I trekked deep into the woods. The trees leaned over me with every step, concealing me from the outside. My children, as ferine as they were, cowered in their own form of unease. The fury that radiated from my bones made the ground tremble. Keres was the only one to approach. She consumed a portion of my anger, shadowing my frenzied movements. The other creatures gathered near, curious of their mother's pain.

"They are weak, Keres," I spoke, gliding my fingers through her fur. "If only these pitiful creatures realized the sacrifice that came with greatness at the start of their incessant begging. They simply cannot handle it. Each one fails and each one dies."

All the whispers of my children's voices hit my ears. They urged for bloodshed. I couldn't have agreed more. After all, it was the purest form of revenge. I was engulfed in a circle of their remarkable malformations and enticing words. And that's when I heard it: the voice of my master. He encouraged me all the same as they did. He wanted me to put an end to the obstacle that Tucker was. But for this, I would need to acquire great patience.

Master told me of the boy's future whereabouts. It was

set in stone; he was bound to return to the forest. My children and I would wait as a spider waits for prey to reach its web. But his would not be any casual death, no, it would be ghastly.

"Oh, foolish, foolish," I announced, "The boy has sentenced himself to *death!*"

The beasts cheered through horrendous roars and cackles, awaiting the downfall of another one of God's children.

I went to the tree that was once my bane and my rescuer. Its leaves were the darkest shade of red they had ever been. They had been stained to their core with the blood of all those souls my children had consumed. I placed my hand against its dreadfully cold skin and peered up at the sky. Once again, the eyes of the angels scowled at me. I laughed uncontrollably at their glimmering faces, knowing all they could do was watch. And then, with one sudden burst, I let out a scream so mighty that it released a bolt of red into the sky. It was meant as a celebration of my own, but also as a warning to the rest of the world. I knew they would not hear it or see it because they have always been so absent to our existence, which only made it better. Though this absence would not last much longer. Our glory would scourge the Earth.

~ 19 ~

TUCKER

It was only my third night of work, yet I was dreading it. And you might say, "Weren't you already dreading it?" Well, yes. But now, Shiloh knew something wasn't right. This gave her all the more reason to put me on her kill list. And at 17 years old, I wasn't exactly ready to die yet.

I tried to act as normal as possible when I got there, but it didn't last long. I saw Shiloh in the greenhouse while I was picking up my usual security items, but she didn't say a single word to me. I got one cold glance from her and that was it for the entire night. The one thing that worried me more was that the large figure I had seen in the greenhouse earlier that week was no longer there. The inside of the structure looked as though it had been recently tidied up. That meant whatever monstrosity she had been building was now free to roam. I couldn't help but think that she had created it just to kill me. Yes, I know, how narcissistic of me, right?

The night started off without any issues. Hundreds of

people wandered mindlessly into the forest, laughing and having a good time. A few seconds after they entered, my whole body would tense, waiting to hear the sound of their screams. I now questioned if each scream I heard in the past was just from a person getting spooked or because they were about to be eaten alive by the demented freaks Shiloh kept in there. But the screams only lasted for a short time.

For hours, nothing happened, nothing at all. It was like the monsters in the trees had all gone to sleep and every person who walked through had just wasted $20 on a ticket. For once, my heart stayed beating at a fairly normal rate.

After some time, there had been a pause in customers and I was growing antsy. Walking the same path back and forth wasn't exactly a thrilling experience. Plus, the opportunity just seemed so perfect. I strolled back to the front of the woods where the arch was, expecting to see an empty area. And well, I wasn't completely wrong; there were no people there. But there was something moving. I kept a safe distance as I observed the odd movements coming from the top of the arch. At first, I assumed it was just a large bird or maybe even a stray cat. The thought that I was at a haunted house full of paranormal creatures hadn't even crossed my mind . . . that was until I realized what I was looking at. The gargoyles. I had forgotten about them entirely, but suddenly, there was that intense urge to run in the opposite direction. As if they knew I was looking at them, they simultaneously turned to face me with their red, glowing eyes. They crawled around on the wooden arch like vultures, digging their claws into anything they could grasp and flaunting the strength of their wings. As one continued to climb around, the other stared at me relentlessly. I tried to show my courage by staring back, but that only made things worse. The gargoyle grinned widely. It knew my face and it knew my fears. And if it really wanted to, it could use those fears against me. I had a feeling it was going to. In fact, it already was.

I hid myself behind the thicket of the trees, blocking the gargoyle's view, but I still couldn't get its grinning face out of my head.

Just then, the noises began. A rumbling howl sounded from somewhere in the woods. My head shot in the direction of the sound. Then, multiple guttural cries rang out from various areas. There were too many to trace. I could feel my breathing getting more intense. The sounds turned into a rhythm. A branch would snap and a beast would wail, then another would yelp, and another would shriek. The sounds became endless. I wrapped my arms around my head tightly, trying to cover my ears. I squinted into the darkness, looking for any sight of the things that were making the noises, but I never saw anyone or anything. The endless cries continued, gradually getting louder and shaking the ground as if they were all closing in on me. My lungs heaved for air, but it was stolen by the dark night around me. Suddenly, as my eyes darted around, the trees crept closer. I wanted to run, but I couldn't move. My feet were cemented into the dirt. The roots of the trees crawled up my legs and held me firmly in place as everything around me grew dark. There was no light left for my eyes to hold onto. Oddly enough, the howls of the beasts died out and it seemed to be silent, but as I let my arms drift slowly away from my ears, all those noises I had heard were now whispers. The voices were sharp and painful to listen to, but I had no other choice as the roots snatched my arms as well. They held me there and made me endure their horrible taunts. And then, their eyes appeared to me. No faces, just the eyes . . . all of them. I had never experienced anything so utterly terrifying up until that moment. All the hope I once had was now drained from my body. I felt like I was dying. Maybe I was.

All of a sudden, everything stopped. There were no more eyes or whispers or roots. I just saw a black screen from behind my tightly sealed eyes. The last thing I wanted to do was open them, but I had to. They cautiously fluttered open and the setting around me was back to normal. I saw the trees I had been hiding behind, the night sky up above me, and the front entrance just over the hill with gleaming lights. Now, I was positive this place was evil. I had to leave. Yet, as sure as I was about my decision, I felt the desperate need to look back at those gargoyles one last time. And sure enough, they were perched on top of the arch, full of life. Their wings flapped chaotically as they guarded the entrance, but they no longer seemed to care so much about me.

Then, just as I was about to leave, I got a completely different feeling in my chest. It was a familiar feeling, a safe feeling, one that only God can provide. As if He held a hand out towards me and guided my chin, I turned my head to look into the forest. A faint beam of light streamed down from deep within the shadowy trees and cast a flash of radiance onto something that lay on the ground. It turned out, that "something" was a person – a corpse to be more specific. Their blood splattered the dirt beneath them and ghastly wounds were carved deeply into their face and torso. I didn't know how to react. I couldn't scream or else I would end up just like they did. Instead, I booked it for the front entrance of the property, not caring who saw me. My legs have never pushed harder in all my life. I raced into the greenhouse, picked up my things, and headed straight for my bike. As I ran, I ripped the serpent necklace right off and tossed it carelessly into the dirt, never wanting to see it again.

By a miracle of God, there were no more customers waiting to get in, just a bunch of Shiloh's freaks working the booths. And thankfully, Shiloh was nowhere to be seen. I ignored all the workers and pedaled away from that horrid place without ever looking back.

Once I finally got home, I paced outside for a few minutes before entering. I didn't know what to do with myself. Part of me thought I should call the cops but another part of me thought Shiloh would immediately have me killed if I did that.

But all of those thoughts disappeared when the front door suddenly swung open. I jumped, looking like a deer in headlights.

"Tucker!" my father shouted angrily. He looked like he was fuming as his hand tightly grasped the door. Just then, he stomped down the front step and grabbed me by the arm before I had any time to react. "Get your ass in that fucking house right now."

I tried to push him off of me, but the more I fought, the tighter his grip got. I knew I'd have a ring of bruises around my arm the next day.

"You sneaky little fuck," he grumbled, dragging me through the house.

My mom was waiting in the kitchen with her arms folded, wearing the same clothes she had probably been wearing since the day before. Her face was just as angry while she watched our scuffle, but I still couldn't understand why. Unfortunately, I found out very quickly.

My dad led me all the way to my room at the end of the hall and threw me at the cracked open door. It burst open as I fell into it, slamming against my wall. I scurried around on the floor for a moment, taking in what just happened, and when I saw my dad looming in the doorway, I quickly stood up. My whole body was shaking as I backed up into a corner of my room.

"What the hell is this?" My dad picked up a stack of money that was lying on my bookshelf and shook it in my face. He crumpled the money tightly in his hand and started to move towards me.

I tried to back up more but there was nowhere else to go.

"Is this from that little job of yours? You didn't care to tell us you were making $400 a week?" he shouted. His head was getting so red that I could see the veins popping in his neck. "No, of course not! Instead, you tried to hide it from us!"

Then, my mom showed up behind him. Her arms were still folded, but now, she decided to join in on the screaming. Neither of them felt the need to keep their voices down because we didn't have any next-door neighbors, but even if we did, nobody would call the cops. It was usual for the bad part of town we lived in to have parents like mine.

My mom's voice was practically deafening. "Do you realize how hard we work to keep this house running? If you're going to be making money then you have to pay rent! We own this house and with all we've done for you-"

"What have you done for me?" I finally yelled.

They both looked at me in shock.

"Please," I shifted my watery gaze between them, "Tell me what exactly it is that you've done for me. Because the way I see it, I have had to raise myself ever since Tessa left. You tossed us both to the side like we were some terrible burden your whole lives. I don't owe you anything." I did my best to keep my voice calm and steady, but the oncoming tears made it difficult.

I think for a split second, reality hit my parents. But it didn't last very long because they didn't want to accept reality. Ever. That would require them to also accept that they were wrong. But they were always right and they knew better than me. I couldn't do anything about it.

"How dare you," my father spoke in a disturbingly quiet voice. It was the calm before the storm. He was about to get a whole lot worse. There wasn't anything I could use nearby to protect me if he got violent again, which I knew he would. "You and Tessa would've died without us. We gave you food. We put clothes on your back!"

"Oh, congratulations! You did the bare minimum as parents! Do you even hear yourselves? You never should've even been allowed to have kids!"

My mom stepped closer, raising her finger at me. "Your sister was a sneaky little bitch! She pulled the same routine as you and look what happened. If you don't want to end up like her then you are going to split that money!"

Out of my own anger, I got closer to her as well. We were face to face, spitting at each other like two rabid dogs. "I earned that money for myself! So that I could escape this hellhole since neither of you were ever going to help me! You think I enjoy being here?"

I was so caught up in arguing with my mom, that I hadn't even seen my dad approach. In the blink of an eye, I was on the ground with blood pouring out of my nose. All it took was that final comment for them to throw me out of the house altogether. They tossed most of my clothes outside with me, along with some hygiene essentials, but that was it. The one important thing they forgot was my money. They kept that for themselves.

~ 20 ~

TUCKER

I woke up the next morning on Asher's couch. I had called him the previous night about my parents kicking me out and he immediately offered to let me stay with him for as long as I needed. Surprisingly, his parents were more than happy to have me. They had never had two kids in the house so it was an interesting change for them. Although, I didn't want to be a burden so I knew I would try and stay out of their house as much as possible. In fact, I hadn't even had a bite to eat when I left. I had a moral obligation to call the cops and tell them about the body. I told Asher everything beforehand so he was able to cover for me if his parents decided to ask any questions.

Knowing the negligence of the cops in our town, I made my way down to the haunted house to check if they even showed up. To my surprise, they were already there when I arrived. As I pedaled along the wooden fence, I watched two of them talk to Shiloh at the front entrance. She seemed oddly calm considering someone had reported seeing a dead body on her property. The moment I got within sight, Shiloh's gaze met my own. She watched me bike into the parking lot without ever looking away. The dark expression in her eyes told me that she knew I was the one who had called the police before my name was ever brought up.

The two men turned to look at me when they heard the skid of my bike in the dirt. Neither one of them looked nearly qualified for their job. One was a scrawny old man with bright white hair who looked like he was a single cough away from death. The other was a balding, fat guy who probably couldn't catch a snail. They both shared the same grumbled expression on their faces like it was such a chore to actually do their jobs for once.

"Who are you?" the old one questioned in a shaky voice.

The fat one put his hands on his belt, trying to seem more intimidating. His face was full of arrogance.

"I'm the one who called," I answered, trying not to look at Shiloh, although I could feel her eyes watching me non-stop.

"Ha, of course," the fat cop chuckled sarcastically.

I glared at him. The smug look on his face told me everything I needed to know.

"Looks like you were right, Ms. Farrington," he grinned at Shiloh, "Just some stupid kid who doesn't have a damn clue what he's talking about."

I shifted my disgust between the three of them as they laughed. "Officers, I'm not lying. I was here last night. My job is to patrol the perimeter of the haunt. I saw it, I saw a dead body in there," I spoke readily.

Just then, the two officers glanced at me differently. All their pride had washed away for a moment.

"Wait, wait, wait," the fat one put a hand up, "You work here?" He now looked confused.

I nodded. "Yes, I-"

"No," Shiloh interjected. Her eyes stared me down coldly. "He *used* to work here."

"What?" I furrowed my brow.

"Mr. Romero was fired last night after a . . . an *altercation*," Shiloh said with a fake smile. It was clear she already had the upper hand and she was going to do anything to win the cops over. And from the looks of it, she had already won. "He was gone before the night even began. His feet never crossed farther than the greenhouse."

The two men nodded along with her false story, not that they really knew any better; they were already lacking brain cells.

"So, you're mad you got fired after some stupid argument and then you decide to make a story about this poor woman? What kind of sick bastard lies like that?" the old guy frowned. He looked me up and down like any older person does when they think they're talking to a senseless teenager.

"Sir, with all due respect, that's not what happened. She's lying to you. She's lied about everything. A-and I'm not the only one to accuse her of something like this. Don't you think the coincidences have run out by now?" I just stood there, foolishly trying to prove my point that they would never believe.

They scowled at me like I had no idea what I was saying.

Shiloh had them wrapped around her finger, and all it took was a charming smile and some batting of the eyes.

The officers began to walk off towards their cars, making snide comments about me as they went.

"Did you guys even search the forest at all?" I spoke up one last time, waving my arms around out of desperation.

The fat one stopped in his tracks and peered back at me. "Kid, there's no need for that. We know what happened. Now you're just wasting our time. Leave this woman alone and go find yourself a new job at a grocery store or something."

"But-"

He dismissed me with his hand and trudged back to his car. The two of them sped out of the parking lot without a care in the world about the truth. They made a joke out of their jobs. Nothing about them upheld justice or safety, just a crappy reputation that got them paid.

"That was an adorable attempt, Tucker. If only those men carried a little bit of intelligence with them, you might have actually gotten somewhere with that story of yours," Shiloh hissed from behind me.

I turned sharply. For the first time, I wasn't afraid of her; I was just angry. "They're going to find out what you are. The whole world's gonna know," I stated, looking her directly in the eyes.

"And how is it that you plan on going about exposing me? The boys in blue don't seem to care. And yet, they're the ones who are supposed to be protecting children like you," she sneered. She had quickly lost her pleasant smile that she had been parading around for the past few minutes. "Or, are you going to tell the Big Man in Charge?" she whispered, looking up at the sky. "But no. He doesn't seem to care either. He has abandoned you, Tucker. You can even try and run to your parents, but wait!" She touched her tongue to the roof of her mouth mockingly. "Just like your God, they have abandoned you as well. They *all* have. I was the only one who did not. I protected you. I provided you with wealth. I gave you a second chance at survival. And you threw it back in my face!"

I broke the ties to her mental manipulation with each word she spoke. There was no more time for me to believe anything she was saying.

"Now, boy, you are an even easier target than you were before. My children will take you to our master. You cannot escape him. No matter how much you prepare, no matter how hard you fight, he will have you." Her voice contained the voices of a thousand others. They were all there at that moment. They sought fear and panic. But they got none. And it pissed them off big time.

"No matter how much you prepare," I mocked, "No matter how hard you fight," a smirk formed on my face, "My God will not let any of that happen. But good luck," I grinned widely with a slight sneer. This sense of confidence that overcame me was unrecognizable. It didn't feel like I was the one speaking, but instead, someone higher up.

I turned my back on Shiloh and went back to pick up my bike. I could feel the energy of her anger trying to grab at me as I left. And as I pedaled down the road, I barely had any remembrance of what I had just said to Shiloh, and the feeling of just being a nonsensical teenage boy returned to me.

~ 21 ~

TUCKER

The next couple of weeks leading up to Halloween dragged on and on. Asher and Charli tried to help me keep the haunted house out of my mind, but it didn't work. That place held a sort of mental torment over me that was inescapable.

But I will say, during that time, I was beyond thankful to Asher's family for taking care of me. They had no obligation to take care of me and yet they took me in as if I was already one of their own. It helped Asher and I grow closer than ever before. He even managed to convince me to start going to the gym with him. I always felt like a little kid next to him when we would look in the mirror, but he never made fun of me for it.

Charli would constantly come over since she lived only a few streets down. Her attitude was a lot more positive since I left my job. I guess she was just happy that she didn't have to worry about me getting put in constant danger anymore. She and Asher really did act like my older siblings, and I think they enjoyed it.

My love for Halloween quickly returned when I got to see all the houses lined up with decorations. For a whole month, there were jack-o-lanterns, fake graveyards full of skeletons and tombstones, hanging bats, and giant cobwebs. Although I never really got to experience any of that as a kid, I somehow felt the nostalgia hit me like it does everyone else. To make things even more festive, Charli suggested we all go trick-or-treating for the last time while we were still technically kids. Asher didn't seem too keen on the idea, but once she told him he didn't have to wear some "childish" costume, he quickly changed his mind. Besides, who doesn't want free candy?

We enjoyed soaking up the comfort of autumn for as long as we could. But that all changed on Hallow's Eve.

Halloween fell on a Saturday that year, so everyone was already mentally checked out during school on Friday. Our school went all out on decorations, which was expected considering we lived in one of the spookiest cities in the country. Being a resident of Sleepy Hollow automatically made you fall in love with October.

Everyone was running through the hall, buzzing with excitement and impatience. My last class of the day was probably the worst. It was full of all those obnoxiously loud kids that unfortunately fit into that high school stereotype. You know what I'm talking about. Anyways, while they were sitting in the back of the room chattering like a pack of hyenas, I eavesdropped from my corner seat, farthest from the door. My history teacher knew she couldn't control us, so she basically let us run wild for the entire period.

I kept to myself for most of the time, drawing random doodles in my notebooks out of boredom. Nobody ever spoke to me in that class. It's not that they hated me or thought I was weird, they just had closer friends there that they would rather talk to. I understood that. If I was with Asher and Charli, I'd be doing the same thing. So it was a mutual respect, and I preferred it that way. Asher and Charli were in math, but I knew they were still having more fun than me. But then, my boredom suddenly disappeared when I heard one of my classmates bring up something that sparked my interest.

"What about Soul of the Wilderness?" one of the girls asked. Her name was Lydia. She was a royal you know what. Charli would always joke that people would only hang out with the girl because she forced them to be friends with her. At first, I thought it was mean, but the more I watched how Lydia behaved, it made perfect sense. She looked plain, but at the same time, she clearly gave off that mean girl energy.

Another girl, Jolene, nodded in agreeance, yet she almost seemed bored of her "friends" around her. Jolene was practically a clone of Lydia, just a lot quieter. Instead of saying her rude opinions out loud all the time, she usually just kept them in her head, which was made clear based off her constantly changing facial expressions.

The last girl was Abbie. "Yes! I can't wait!" she shouted in response to Lydia. She was the definition of ditsy. As much as I could hardly tolerate any of them, she was the most likable. Abbie typically just talked your ear off with whatever nonsense she could, but she could definitely be mean if she wanted to.

And then, there were the two guys: Austin and Luke. I was pretty sure that they were just there for the female attention. They both responded to Lydia's question by nodding with a casual, "Yeah, for sure." It was obvious they hadn't heard a thing any of the girls were talking about.

I had been friends with Luke a few years back, but he moved on when he got to high school. To the rest of them, I was really just an acquaintance.

"What time should we get there?" Lydia continued.

I leaned forward in my seat, trying to get a closer listen.

"Hmm," Luke thought aloud. His eyebrows drew close together under his sandy blonde hair as he thought. He had one of those side-swept, fringe haircuts that he always had to flip out of his face just to be able to see. "I think we should get there early to see the performance."

Performance? What performance?

"Oh yeah! I wanna see the little concert thingy too," Abbie added.

What were they talking about? Did Shiloh book a band for the final night? I tried to think of all the possibilities, but nothing made sense. As usual, my curiosity overtook me. "Hey, Luke?" I spoke up.

He spun around with a blank expression that soon turned into a friendly smile when he realized it was me. "What's up, Tuck?" His face was still the same as when we were kids. He had that recognizable, goofy smile that somehow made all the girls blush.

But when I saw that smile, I could remember us sitting in a sandbox at his house playing with toy trucks and whatever bugs we could find. His mom would always yell at him to keep the sand out of his hair because it was the same color.

"Did you say that Soul of the Wilderness is having a concert?" I asked nervously while his friends all stared me down in the background.

"Yeah," he glanced back at his friends, "It's like some sort of show that the owner is doing for Halloween night. I'm not completely sure," he said, looking back at his group again for some more answers.

Jolene rolled her eyes at Luke for his vague explanation. "It's just some big freakshow performance. I think she's bringing out some actors on stage to entertain us before we can enter the haunted house," she explained. Although her tone was blunt, Jolene was actually being quite nice. And those had probably been the most words she'd ever said to me during our entire 11 years of school together.

"I had no idea she was doing that . . ." I veered off quietly. There was no plausible explanation in my head for why Shiloh would put on such a big event.

"Yeah, neither did we. I guess it's a new thing this year," Jolene mumbled, staring at her phone.

Then it hit me. This wasn't some new, grand tradition that Shiloh was starting for her business. It was the end. And she wanted to go out with a bang. Whatever was going to happen at that "show" definitely wasn't going to be good.

Time ticked on slowly in that class and my brain grew bored. I stared at my desk for what felt like hours.

As soon as that last bell rang, I ran to find my friends. People gave me dirty looks as I barreled through them down the hall. Just then, I caught a glimpse of Charli's chocolate brown ponytail swaying through the masses of random heads.

"Charli!" I shouted above all the noise of bustling people.

She didn't seem to hear me. I called again, but she just kept walking. I began shoving through more aggressively. It felt like everyone was purposely trying to move in front of me.

When I finally caught up to Charli, I put a hand on her shoulder to get her attention. As she turned to face me, I realized something was extremely wrong. She had a deranged smile spread widely across her face and her eyes were snake-like. I ripped my hand away in shock.

"*It's too late, Tucker,*" she sang. The voice wasn't hers. It wasn't Shiloh's either. It sounded demonic. "*He's going to take you. He's going to take you.*" The slits in her eyes dilated until they turned fully black.

It was like staring into the eyes of death. I took a few steps back, trying to stop my body from completely freezing up.

"*You can't survive. You can't survive. You can't survive,*" she repeated over and over. This demented lookalike of Charli refused to lose the smile. Her lips were stretched so tightly over her lips that it seemed like they were going to start bleeding.

I spun around on my heels and ran in the opposite direction. All the people had somehow disappeared and I was sprinting down an empty hallway. The more I pushed, the longer the hall got. It stretched into an endless abyss, the lights flickering above me. I glanced over my shoulder to see the evil version of Charli right behind me, also running. If I stopped, she'd catch me, but if I kept going, there would be no end.

"Help!" I screamed, hoping the hand of God would pluck me out of that hellish nightmare. I ran and ran, even when my lungs felt like they were going to fail. But then, as I took another peek behind me, my ankle gave way. My face and hands hit the icy cold floor. Everything was pitch black for a minute and I couldn't move. When I finally lifted my head, I saw a desk in front of me. I was still sitting in my history class, but I was the only one besides my teacher at the front, who was busy packing up her bag to leave.

"Tucker," a voice called from the doorway.

Still disoriented, I looked to see Asher and Charli standing in the door. They gave me funny looks as I stared at them blankly.

"Come on," Charli giggled, wondering why I was acting so strange.

I cautiously stood up and grabbed my backpack. As I approached, I examined both of their faces closely. They seemed perfectly normal.

"What's wrong with you?" Asher tilted his head with puzzlement.

I shook my head. "I don't know. I must've fallen asleep

or something," I mumbled, hoping they'd change the subject. The truth is, I knew it wasn't just a dream and I definitely hadn't fallen asleep. Shiloh was tormenting me, putting visions in my head. She still had some sort of connection to me that allowed her that power. I didn't tell Asher and Charli because I didn't need them to be more freaked out than they already were about the whole situation. But I did need to tell them about my classmates.

"Freedom at last," Charli murmured as we pushed through the school doors into the open air.

The two of them were going to walk on normally, but I stopped. They looked back at me in confusion.

"Guys. We have to go back to the haunted house," I said.

The look of horror on their faces was immediate.

"What?" Charli squinted. "You're joking, right? Like, you can't actually be serious."

Asher's eyes filled with worry all over again. "Tuck . . ."

"I heard people in my class talking about it. They're going there tomorrow night and they said there's some sort of show going on."

Charli tilted her head back and took a deep breath when the realization hit her. I could tell she was already coming up with an excuse for us not to go back.

"Who was talking about it?" Asher questioned. He seemed open to ideas, but it was going to be hard to convince him.

"Lydia's group."

"Oh, oh, of course," Charli laughed sarcastically. There was clear irritation in her voice. "You're going to have us risk our asses for *her*?"

Asher and I sighed simultaneously.

"Shiloh could literally kill them," I made my voice stronger, "And if there's any chance we can stop that from happening, then don't you think we should at least try?"

Asher rolled his eyes, not in a rude way, but more like a "your attitude is killing me" type of way. He looked at Charli with forced sympathy. "As much as you don't like her-" he paused.

I raised my eyebrows at him, hinting for him to correct himself.

He pursed his lips out of realization. "As much as you don't like *any of them*," he grinned, "They're still human beings. Would you really want them to get murdered?"

We both folded our arms, awaiting Charli's snarky response. And just like that, we got one.

"I'm not gonna answer that question," she said straight-faced, folding her arms to mimic us.

"Okay, well, it's two versus one, so we're going," Asher stated bluntly. "Think about it. We're the only ones who know about the crazy stuff that's happening there and nobody else is going to believe us until they see it for themselves. But by then it will be too late. So . . ." he sighed, "Now we just have to figure out a way to keep ourselves alive too." His eyes landed on me, expecting a solution.

My thoughts ran blank for a moment. I didn't know why I hadn't thought of a plan beforehand. "We sneak in, I guess. Then, take it from there," I blurted out.

Charli glared at me, mouth agape. "Oh yeah, that's a great plan. We might as well light ourselves on fire while we're at it," she said sarcastically, rolling her eyes.

I shrugged. "I'm sorry. There's not much we can do. It's a game of chance at this point. So, we can either do our best to save them, or we can cower and let them all walk straight into their deaths."

Standing with a grumpy hunch, Charli glanced at Asher, waiting for him to say something. I knew that she would come around; it just took the final word from him. He smirked, causing her to let out an irritated huff.

"Fine! We'll go help them," she frowned. Then, she shook her finger at me, "But if you get us killed-"

I stuck my hands up humorously. "I won't."

She gave one last scowl and got on her bike, ready for us all to leave.

"Hopefully," I murmured under my breath, just loud enough for Asher to hear.

He gave a half-grin, his nerves poking through.

We were all far too relaxed about the whole thing and I knew that. But I preferred to enjoy life to the best of my ability while I still could, because soon enough, we'd be experiencing hell on Earth, literally.

$$\sim 22 \sim$$

TUCKER

On the day of Halloween, I expected utter chaos to be surrounding me at every moment. But somehow, life was still. The day went by slowly as my friends and I prepared ourselves for night to take over. We spent quite a bit of time in the abandoned church, praying to just make it through the night. Except, knowing what we were going up against, it was definitely a lot to ask for.

When the sun finally set and the clock hit seven, it was time for us to leave. Each step I took towards Asher's front door was strained with apprehension. The more I thought about it, the more I became convinced that I *was* losing my mind. How could three kids possibly take down some demonic witch and her forest full of monsters?

Even as we traveled down the road, I could tell that the sky above us was full of angry storm clouds. Thunder bellowed through them and eventually, they would send down a single, sporadic bolt of lightning as if to warn us all. And yet, not a single drop of rain ever fell. Perhaps the subtle pitter-patter would have distracted from the fact that the sky was growling with anticipation. The Earth was preparing for a war, an ugly war.

The whole ride there was miserable. Not one of us could muster a smile. We were all trapped in our own heads with thoughts that terrified us. I knew Shiloh would use those thoughts against us. She had already brought them to life – molded them with her hands. And they were waiting for us.

From about a mile down the road, we could already see the colorful, ambient glow that the haunted house put off. Rays of purple and orange shot into the sky, reflecting off of the low-hanging clouds. If I hadn't known what was really happening there, I would've thought it was beautiful just like everyone else. But my perception had been poisoned with the unwelcome truth. I knew that once you entered those gates at the entrance, there was a strong chance you would never walk back out. I was now one of those people and so were my friends. I put them in danger because of my own stupid decisions and now it was time to own up to it. Other than the physical things that scared me, like all of Shiloh's creatures, that's the one thing that haunted me the most; I never wanted to lose Asher and Charli. They were the only real family I had left.

"Are you guys sure about this?" I asked them as we approached the parking lot.

They looked back at me with expressions I had never wished to see. There was acceptance on both of their faces, acceptance of fate.

"We have to, Tuck. Because like you said, if we just sit

by, knowing it will happen . . ." Charli shook her head, "Then *we* basically contributed to the murder of dozens of people. I don't want that on my conscience," she said, her eyes filling with sorrow.

I took one deep breath and led the way towards the entrance. We left our bikes by the fence as a quick get-away, although we weren't sure if it would be necessary at all. For the most part, we blended in with the rest of the crowd just fine, besides the fact that our eyes were darting every which way in fear of being spotted. The line moved faster than usual. It felt like they were shoving people in as quickly as possible, but not for our satisfaction, instead, for a very bad reason.

Once we got past the ticket booth, we entered a carnival-like area. I guess I had never seen what it was like up close before. There was so much to look at that my brain could hardly focus. People bustled around in excitement as they examined the elaborate array of decorations and dressed-up freaks. Eerie music blasted from the many speakers that were placed all around us; they sat in every corner and above all of our heads. Kids ran by with mouths full of cotton candy and popcorn like it was some sort of circus. With all the different sensory details, it felt like I wasn't actually there. It felt like a dream. I looked up at the lights and realized that we were trapped in a box. The lights were the ceiling, the people were the walls, and the vibration of the music was the floor beneath our feet. That was Shiloh's trick; she made it look and feel like any other festive attraction you would go to, but this one wasn't just some money grabber.

Within minutes of trying to find our way around the place, we got shoved along with the crowd towards the mini stage which no longer seemed to be so mini. That demented clown was back and he was dancing around on the stage without saying a word, much like a mime. The people were fascinated by him and his little magic tricks he would occasionally do. The lights flickered and flashed to the changes of the music as he performed, but his deranged smile, well, that never changed. In fact, neither did his eyes. Yes, there were lots of people in front of me who would block my view every now and then, but from what I saw, that clown never blinked.

All of a sudden, the music went dead silent and so did the crowd. The lights on the stage went completely dark, clouding everyone's vision. I felt Asher and Charli move closer to me in a frightened panic. For a few seconds, it seemed like there had been a major power outage, but then, the stage lights shot back on. It was almost as blinding as the sun. As the brightness slowly faded back to normal, the lone outline of a tall, thin, female figure appeared. With her hands raised elegantly in the air, Shiloh's face became visible. And for the first time ever, she carried a huge smile across her face, showing off her perfect white teeth; they were practically shimmering under the light.

"Welcome, ladies and gentlemen, boys and girls," she spoke charismatically into the microphone, grinning even wider. Her piercing green eyes traveled through the many faces in the crowd. "How lovely it is to see you all here tonight. I'm *so glad* you could make it." Her presenter voice was so phony that it almost seemed real.

Out of the corner of my eye, I noticed a police officer standing near one of the concession stands. I nudged my friends and discreetly led them through the mass of people as Shiloh continued with her announcements.

"Is there really only one cop here?" Charli said in a hushed voice as we escaped the crowd.

"Seems like it," Asher mumbled as we approached the man.

I thought it was obvious that three kids walking directly toward the cop in a hasty manner would've gotten his attention, but the cop didn't even look our way. His eyes were focused on the stage, just like everybody else.

"Excuse me," I spoke up, waving my hand politely.

He just looked on in silence. It wasn't that loud that he couldn't hear me. I could see Charli and Asher giving me concerned glances from behind. I peered down to read the nametag on his chest pocket. It read: **Officer Holt**. He was a strong-looking, young guy with a fresh haircut and great height. Everything about him seemed a little too perfect.

I took a step closer. "Excuse me, offic- uh- Officer Holt," I said loudly.

He didn't even bother to look at us when he said, "Shh. You're going to miss the best part." His gaze was stuck on Shiloh.

She was eerily still as she stared down everyone in sight. Admittedly, she looked gorgeous standing there with her bright smile and elegant clothing, but it was all a trick. Suddenly, she whipped around and walked towards the back of the stage, her face hidden from our view. Out of nowhere, there was a puff of green flames that engulfed her entire body, yet they didn't seem to burn her skin. She turned back around and threw her hands into the air dramatically, revealing her new face. The skin around her eyes and mouth was tarnished with complete darkness that shot off like bolts of lightning to other parts of her face. Her eyes stuck out even more now, giving off their luminous emerald glow. The darkness coated her hands as well and sporadically spread up her arms like vines on a wall. It almost looked like she had been painted with ashes. The crowd cheered wildly for her transformation. They had no idea.

"Sir, you have to get these people out of here," I urged, keeping one eye on Shiloh at all times.

The officer finally turned his head to look at me. I recoiled back slightly when I saw the same sort of evil illusion in his eyes. His irises were so pale that they nearly glowed. It looked like he was wearing costume contacts, but I knew he wasn't. He gave us the same deranged smile that the clown had. "Get them out? It's too late for that," the man spoke in a disturbing tone.

The three of us cautiously backed away, but remained entranced by his eyes nonetheless. He didn't seem aggressive in any way, but instead, he turned back to watch Shiloh on the stage.

"We have to get her away from them," Asher said frantically.

"But how?" Charli cried out. Her voice was starting to get shaky with panic. That never happened to Charli. "They're not gonna listen to us. We-"

"I have an idea," I interjected. A surge of adrenaline

ran through my veins and I took off towards the back of the stage.

"Wait! Tucker!" Charli shouted over the bustle of people swarming around her and Asher.

"Go find Lydia's group!" I yelled, taking a quick glance back at their panicked faces among the crowd of people. "Go!"

I found my way to the wings of the stage and paused. I watched Shiloh parade around with the microphone in hand, lighting occasional green flames from her fingertips.

"And now," she announced smoothly, "I would like you to meet some of my greatest accomplishments. I went to great lengths to create these certain . . . *costumes*. It only feels proper to share their beauty with you all." Her words echoed throughout the whole property as a hush went over the crowd.

In the other wing, I noticed her freaks standing by, waiting to be introduced. These creations seemed antsy to be released to the public, twitching and pacing. They had the most detailed and eerie designs I had ever seen. I could only imagine the ones that I hadn't been able to see lurking in the woods while on duty.

Shiloh brought the microphone closer to her black lips and a smirk appeared. "Welco-"

"Wait!" I shouted, running onto the stage with my arms waving in the air.

Everyone either looked puzzled or disgusted. Whispers began to travel throughout the crowd, various comments hitting my ears. Shiloh was stunned. She tried to keep up her "friendly" smile for the customers, but the rage in her eyes was all I saw.

"This woman has trapped all of you! She plans to kill you! She is not a normal person! The stories are true!" I announced.

The expression of every single person there made me feel like an idiot. They glared at me as though I had just ruined their whole night.

My forehead began to run with sweat. "I'm telling you the truth! I've seen what she's capable of-"

"You're ruining the show!" a random voice shouted.

"Get down!"

"Get off the stage!"

As I stood there in an utter panic, not knowing what to do, I saw Asher and Charli's faces off to the side. They shared my despair as they watched me in silence. Alongside them were all the members of Lydia's group. That was just about the only thing that gave me comfort in that moment.

Shiloh took the mic away from her mouth. "Tucker," she grinned widely, "I thought I warned you to never come back. And yet here you are."

Worried creases formed on my brow. I tried to hold my ground for as long as possible, but I could feel myself cowering under Shiloh's gaze. "You're not going to hurt these people," I voiced.

"Oh, but it's too late for that. I already have." Her eyes narrowed as she moved towards me. "Just by them being here, I have separated them from their God. They belong to me now."

I peered into the crowd, trying to find Asher and Charli's faces, but they were gone. "No," I began to sputter, taking frightened steps backward.

All of a sudden, Officer Holt appeared from the stage wing, taking urgent steps toward me.

"No," I repeated, looking wildly into the crowd of people. I searched and searched for my friends, but they were nowhere to be seen. I felt Officer Holt's cold hands wrap around my arms and begin to drag me off the stage. The faces all blurred together to form one. That face became Shiloh's, and then Holt's, and then a screen of dark nothingness.

CHARLI

I remember meeting Tucker Romero for the first time in eighth grade, and I am so grateful I did. He always hung around Asher, and boy did they make a funny team. Most of the people at our school would just ignore them because they were more of the quiet type, but so was I. Those same people never even gave us the time of day to say hello, not even once. So, I guess, that drew me to Tucker and Asher. It might sound a little weird, but I would often observe how they interacted during English. They were like brothers, but not the kind that got in constant fights, these two were the kind that would give their life just so the other could have a chance at happiness. I liked to listen to all the jokes they would make from the back of the classroom, no matter how bad they were sometimes. Their bond was something I hadn't seen in anyone else. It was no wonder everyone thought those two were blood-related upon meeting them.

Tucker always stuck out to me in a different way

though. He acted so freely around Asher, but any time a teacher or anyone older than him would approach, he turned into a completely different person and would hide his personality. It was like he thought he was about to be scolded at any moment for having fun or even just for speaking. It wasn't until Tucker rolled up his sleeves one day that I started to realize what was actually going on with the poor kid. He had bruises all over his arms and as soon as he realized his mistake, he immediately pulled the sleeves back down. The more I watched him over the course of the year, the worse it seemed to get. Some days it was pretty obvious that he was in pain or had recently been crying before showing up to class. There were even a few occurrences where he had bruises on his face, typically it was a black eye or a mark near his jaw. Although I had never even spoken to him at that point, I felt a deep need to protect him. I had two younger siblings and I knew that if anyone ever tried to hurt them, especially our parents, I wouldn't hesitate to fight back.

One day, as a gift from God, the three of us were put in a group together for a project in our English class. I don't really remember what the project was about, but I do remember the looks on Asher and Tucker's faces. Instead of the typical resentful faces I got from other guys, these two seemed to just be fearful. Their shoulders drooped and they hardly made eye contact with me as I went to join their group. For a while, none of us spoke, which gave me that stupid awkward feeling in the pit of my stomach. But finally realizing that I was clearly the most extroverted out of this group of introverts, I took the liberty of introducing myself first. "I'm Charli," I smiled.

They seemed shocked that I turned out to be nicer than I looked, which was understandable because I never really made an effort to appear happy while at school. I didn't like to lie. Plus, the whole school seemed to have this predetermined notion that I was just a bitch with no friends, which I mean, they weren't technically wrong. I just hated everyone there. Sue me.

Neither of them said anything for a long time, which was only making everyone more uncomfortable.

"Usually this is the part where you two introduce yourselves," I said to them.

"Asher."

"Tucker."

In reality, there was no point in introducing ourselves at all because somehow, whether it was through rumors or reputations, we already knew each other's names.

We all nodded and smiled, casually trying to get rid of the awkwardness. That feeling didn't last long because we discovered fairly quickly that we had a lot more in common with each other than we thought. Instead of getting any of our work done that period, we talked about our mutual dislike for school and all the people in it, our incredible talent to fail the easiest of classes, and our hobby of watching the clock tick away until the bell finally rang. Those types of interactions continued into the next class and the one after that and every day after until the last day of school.

The three of us hung out almost every day during the

summer. I will admit that sometimes I would've preferred to have been by myself, but Asher and I knew that Tucker needed us. He needed an escape. I always felt so guilty watching him go back home. Each time I saw that terrified look in his eyes, the indescribable pain that he had to prepare himself for. It wasn't fair. It's not fair for any person, especially any *child*, to have to go through that.

I remember one day in particular when Asher and I were just waiting outside Tucker's house so that we could go grab ice cream. It was supposed to be a good day. It was supposed to be a day that was painless. But I remember sitting on my bike and hearing shouting from inside. Seconds later, there was the sound of objects being thrown. I think a plate or glass might've even shattered. Asher and I didn't know what to do. We sat there and listened to the whole thing take place. Anyways, Tucker came running out of the house in such a hurry that he forgot to even shut the door behind him. With a streak of blood running from his nose, he hopped on his bike and we rode so far away from that place. There was nothing I wanted to do more than give Tucker's parents a taste of their own medicine, but Asher handled that for me once we got to high school.

Something I've admired about Tucker since the day we met was his love for God. Even if every single person in the whole world were against him all at once, he would still choose God over them. I truly believe that the boy's faith is the thing that kept him going. I know that if it were me dealing with his life, I probably would've given up pretty early on. But he didn't. In fact, he was the one who introduced me to God in the first place. I definitely wasn't in the best mental state when I met Him, but things only got better from there. My stubborn attitude about accepting the truth eventually faded, but not because of my own determination, because of Tucker's. He never gave up on me. I was saved. And it was all thanks to Tucker's kind soul.

So, when I say I love that boy like he's my own brother, I mean it. He was the one who taught me to open up, to be patient, and to *always* stand up for those who cannot stand up for themselves. He still chooses to be kind even when the world has been nothing but cruel to him; that is a rare trait. And that is why I could never possibly let him go.

~ 24 ~

ASHER

I remember meeting Tucker Romero for the first time as kids, and I am so grateful I did. Now, I don't really know what exact day we decided to become brothers, but I do know that neither of us could even read at that point. Our parents put us in the same pre-school and we were in the same class from then on. There were times when we could look and act so alike as little kids that people could hardly tell us apart. Especially as an only child, it was nice to have someone like him around. I was never lonely. We used to rough house a little or throw soccer balls at each other's heads, but that was about the most we ever fought. I really can't remember staying mad at him for more than a day. He was my best friend. He still is.

In all honesty, if Tucker were to ever go away or get lost, I would get lost too. Not a soul would hear from me until I found him. We were inseparable from the start, so there's no way I'd let them take that away from us.

As we grew up together, the more I realized how awful

life at home was for him, if you could even call that a home. The older he got, the worse the beatings became. I tried my best to understand why his parents did what they did to him, but even he couldn't come up with an explanation. I was taught by my parents that if someone was hurt I needed to tell an adult I trusted and I suggested that to Tucker many times, but he never did. I thought the teachers would say something once they noticed the marks all over him because I know for a fact that those assholes noticed. But they never said a word about it. I guess they didn't care to put the effort into something that they weren't getting paid for, even if it meant they could've saved a child. Tucker didn't want me telling any-one either. He thought it would just make things worse. So, I did as he requested and I kept my mouth shut for years. But I knew, I always knew, that someday I would get back at his parents for him. I couldn't sit by forever and watch him be abused.

I also remember the day Charli became part of our two-man circle. All the rumors we had heard about her were wrong, or at least, mostly wrong. She was definitely intimidating with her height and the way she walked so confidently around school. Yet, when she talked to Tucker and I for the very first time, she was nothing but kind. We quickly grew to like her and from what we could tell, she liked us too. I think Tucker was always connected to Charli in a different way than I was. He seemed to envision her as his sister, Tessa, who left when he was very young. I met Tessa once or twice but the memories I had of her were very faint. All I know is that she and Charli shared many similar qualities. I guess that's why Tucker opened up to her so quickly; he felt safe. And knowing that Charli would do anything to protect Tucker as well automatically made me trust her.

Once we all got to high school, our bond was so much stronger. We obviously changed in our own ways, but we never abandoned each other. We soon found out that we didn't have many classes together during freshman year, so we had to find a way to hang out after school. On one of our many bike-riding adventures, we came across an old abandoned church. It was a small building that was pretty secluded from the busy areas of town. The moment we entered the structure, we felt at peace and that's when we decided to make it our dedicated hideout. In all the years of going there, nobody else ever found it. It was like our own special little gift from God. I think He knew how much we needed it, how much Tucker needed it.

Speaking of God, I remember asking Tucker how he was so religious when he experienced so much hell in his life. After all, it wasn't like his parents ever introduced him to any sort of faith. At the time, I didn't really understand his answer. But now, as I've gotten older and at least a little bit wiser, I think I'm finally starting to get it. He said to me, "No one ever told me about God and I never needed them to. He came to me on his own. I could tell you the story of the exact moment He touched my heart, but what would be the point? You have to experience that on your own to actually believe it."

By sophomore year, people were no longer confusing Tucker and I for each other. I had gotten a lot taller and put on quite a bit of muscle mass. I tried to get Tucker to go with me to the gym so that he could get stronger and maybe his parents wouldn't see him as such an easy target, but he always said no. I didn't want to push him out of his comfort zone and make him resent me, so I just reminded him that I would be there to help him if he asked. And one day, the perfect opportunity presented itself.

I was tiredly waiting for Tucker on his porch; I would often meet him there early in the morning before school started and then we would go get Charli on our way. That day, he was late. I sat patiently on his front step for a long time, listening to arguing from inside. It seemed pretty calm for a while until the louder noises started. I got up and stood close to the door. Suddenly, I could hear things being thrown around and the scuffling of feet. Both of his parents were shouting furiously at him non-stop. Then, I heard Tucker's voice. He cried out in pain and I knew that they had done something to him. I didn't care what it was or if they even meant to do it on purpose; his painful cry was his way of pleading for help. That protective older brother feeling hit me and I kicked the door with as much force as I needed until it blasted open. The door handle nearly went flying off as I entered. I'll never forget the horrified looks on his parents' faces . . . or the one on Tucker's. They were standing over him while he was on the floor, scooted up against a wall. I remember seeing the blood dripping from his nose and tears in his eyes as he cowered beneath them. I remember the lamp that was knocked over on the floor with its plug ripped from the wall. And I also remember how satisfying it was to beat the ever-loving shit out of Tucker's father. He wasn't expecting it at all, so with the addition of my new strength and height, I dropped him to the ground pretty easily. His mother just stood like a coward in the kitchen while she watched me fight with her husband. The man didn't even get a chance to hit me back. He just laid there as I pummeled him, almost as if he knew that he deserved it. "If you lay another hand on the kid I will not hesitate to have you sick fucks thrown in prison. Do you understand me?" I said to the man. I wasn't big on swearing, but in that moment the words needed to be heard. I saw his slight nod and I finally let him go. He lay there miserably as I put my arm around Tucker's shoulders and we hurried out of the house. Outside, we found Charli waiting for us. Since the door was wide open, she had seen the whole thing from where she was standing.

She looked at me and smiled. "Thank you."

Before getting on our bikes, Tucker hugged me. He had almost never hugged me before that except when we were really little, so I knew how much it meant for someone to stand up for him.

I'm not sure about the verbal or mental abuse, but I know that the physical abuse stopped for a while. Of course, that wouldn't be the end of it, but at least it gave Tucker some peace for a little bit. I know that if I were in his situation, he would have done the exact same thing for me. And that is why I could never possibly let him go.

~ 25 ~

TUCKER

When I finally gained consciousness again, I found my-self deep in the woods. Shiloh's woods. My head shot up from the ground and I scrambled around in the dirt for a second, desperately trying to stand up while still bearing the weight of utter shock. Adrenaline pumped through my body as my eyes wandered the trees surrounding me. I examined the hanging pattern of the few lanterns nearby, but couldn't recognize any of it. That's when I realized I must have been stuck in the dead center of the haunted house.

Right behind me, sat the largest maple tree I had ever seen in my life. It towered over me with a menacing red glow. That was the same moment I noticed the peculiar scent of the tree. It reeked of ash. But that wasn't all. Along with the ash, was something much more foul; there were subtle hints of rot. I didn't dare go any closer to the tree and find out what the smell really was. Instead,

I headed in the opposite direction, making sure each step was silent and slow.

I was no more than 100 feet away from the giant tree when I heard rustling nearby. I dropped to the ground without hesitation, crouching in the tall grass. As I continued to listen, I could feel various little creepy crawlies moving around me and up my legs. Spiders. I hated spiders. But at the time, those things were the least of my problems.

Suddenly, I heard a hushed whisper from the same area as the rustling. "Tucker," it called.

My eyes grew wide. I remained low to the ground, refusing to move. I was so focused on staying still that I wasn't even breathing.

"Tucker," the voice called again, this time slightly louder. It was definitely a female voice. And as I played it back in my mind, it sounded raspy and familiar. "Tuck."

I peeked out from the tips of the grass and saw multiple human shadows slowly shifting through the trees. I saw the slight swing of a ponytail and realized it was Charli I was hiding from. Beside her, I recognized Asher's brawny figure.

"Charli," I called back in a whisper.

Her face lit up when she saw me stand. "Tuck, come on," she said, waving me over to the group in a hurry.

Thankfully, they were all there: Asher, Charli, and everyone from Lydia's group. Most of them seemed too scared to even speak.

"How did you guys get in here? Did they take you too?"

I asked curiously, constantly looking over my shoulder for a pair of unknown eyes.

"No, we just followed the cop. We saw him carry you into the woods and then somehow we got lost at a certain point," Asher explained.

Realization struck me and worry lined my brow. "No, no," I mumbled to myself, shaking my head.

Everyone's faces filled with confusion.

"What? What's wrong?" Charli said, wide-eyed.

"She made it easy for you to get in because she wanted you to be trapped in here too," I told them. My eyes darted to a nearby tree as a new rustling sounded. "We're being hunted."

That one statement made them all strain with fear. We looked every which way, watching each shadow creep towards us. Just then, that sound started back up, and this time, it was getting closer.

"Guys," I stepped back, "Guys we need to go."

Our eyes were all focused on that one spot. Although there was still no visible figure, the rustling from within the trees turned into heavy, fast-paced footsteps that were barreling toward our group.

"We need to go now!" I shouted. I began forcefully shoving them to move, and it didn't take long before we all started running.

We ran through the forest as fast as our legs could carry us, dodging trees and hanging lanterns. I tried to guide us towards what seemed like open, treeless areas, but every time, there were still trees surrounding us. The sound of fast-paced heartbeats was almost as loud as our terrified breaths. The whole place was like an inescapable funhouse, except no one was having fun.

Our running eventually slowed to a jog after a period of silence from behind us. We were exhausted and frightened; the combination was extremely unpleasant.

After nearly a half hour of jogging, we came to a sudden stop. Abbie had fallen to the ground and tears were streaming down her cheeks. She had her hands wrapped tightly around her ankle as Lydia and Jolene tried to comfort her.

"Oh, no, no. We do not have time for this," Charli huffed in an exasperated tone.

Charli was right. Abbie was known to be overdramatic and this was not the time or the place for it.

"Austin, Luke, get her up. We have to keep moving," I said adamantly.

Just as the two boys were reaching down to help her, Abbie let out an angry huff and pushed their hands away. "Keep moving? Are you serious? We've been running for forever and we *still* haven't found a way out!" she cried.

We all tried to shush her to keep her voice down.

"This place is a fucking maze," Abbie continued in that painfully whiny voice of hers as Lydia sat with her on the ground.

Jolene started shaking her head and staring into the trees as if her eyes were locked onto something specific. "It's not a maze," she grimaced, "It's a cage." She then spun around and looked directly at me. "You got us into this mess. Now, how the fuck are we going to get out?"

Charli turned to glare at her. "Watch it," she growled, "It's not his fault."

Jolene immediately backed down and kept on staring into the trees, stubbornly facing away from all of us.

"Well staying here like a bunch of sitting ducks is only going to get us killed sooner, so I say we keep trying," Asher spoke up, breaking the tension. He looked at Austin and Luke. "Guys, get her up," he gestured to Abbie.

They lifted her by both arms while she attempted to place her weight on her other ankle. Once she was stable enough, we began walking in the same direction as before, hoping to find an end to the trees. But just as we started moving, there was an enormous *snap* from up ahead. We froze. The moon backlit trees, and beyond their silhouettes, we caught a glimpse of shadowed movement. The girls in the back started to chatter. Those of us in the front glanced back at them intensely, hoping they'd take the hint.

"Shh. Shut up," Charli whispered, scowling at each of them.

When we turned back to the situation up ahead, it was no longer just an ominous shadow and some noises. Now, there was a beast. A monster. Its gigantic pale figure was illuminated by the moonlight. It gave the impression of an elk, but not one that had been created by God. It was a creature so horrendous that only the hands of the Devil could have possibly made it. This beast was larger than even the werewolf I had previously seen in those woods. The monster's antlers could hardly fit between the spaces of the trees and its hooves were the size of a human head. Its body looked like it had been starved for years; the skin was so emaciated that pieces of it were falling off the bone, revealing the grotesque insides. A person with no insight on the situation might even take pity on the creature after seeing how thin and sickly it appeared. It huffed in the frigid air, releasing visible, hot breaths from its flaring nostrils.

"Oh my gosh," Lydia voiced from behind us, sounding like she was trying to catch her breath.

"Nobody move," Charli whispered through gritted teeth.

Our eyes were intensely focused on the beast as it remained in place. It twitched its ears and shifted its hooves as it listened to the forest. If I hadn't known it was some sort of demonic presence, I might've thought the creature was beautiful in an odd way. From afar, you could see the power it held in its lungs but also the grace of each movement it made.

From behind, we could hear Lydia shifting around. I turned my head slightly to see her taking slow, small steps back, away from the group. Jolene and Abbie just shook their heads at her and mouthed the word "no" over and over again. But of course, in any scenario when you're trying to be quiet, she broke the silence. With one step, her foot landed right on a twig. Its dried-out center snapped right in half, echoing through the trees. The beast twisted its head in our direction and the eyes of death were upon us. Lydia let out a high-pitched scream at the terrifying gaze of the monster and she took off running.

"No! Lydia!" Jolene shouted as Lydia's figure disappeared into the darkness.

The rest of us had no other choice but to do the same as the creature started to chase after us. Luckily, the great size of its antlers slowed the beast down as it hit the trunks of trees and snagged on their branches. The adrenaline kept us moving at full-speed without stopping. I heard some of the others make the mistake of looking back when I heard their screams at the sight of what was after us. Thunderous footsteps crashed from behind us, shaking the leaves of the trees. Soon enough, I realized that besides the light from the moon, we were running in total darkness. The lanterns that had been strung up were all gone, not a trace of them to be found.

As we ran, the beast let out a deafening cry. It reverberated through the woods with so much power that I swear I could feel its force propelling me forward, similarly to an explosion. Not too long after, several more cries were heard from various areas around us, but these were not the same. These sounds weren't nearly as powerful, and yet, they still shook me to my core. They were calling back to the creature chasing us, and they knew exactly where we were.

"Tucker!" Asher shouted from a few feet away. He pointed to something up ahead. And then, he completely stopped running.

I was blinded by the constant outline of towering trees that I hadn't even noticed what he was pointing to, but then I saw it, and I stopped as well. Crawling down from the trees were child-sized figures. From what I could see at a distance, they had ears like bats and swung effort-lessly from the branches. Their eyes lit up all at once, all with the same yellow glow. Our group stayed near to one another as the creatures closed in. They giggled like hyenas at our terror. Now, we were side by side, staring into the demented eyes Shiloh had created.

All of a sudden, a vehement breath sounded from behind us. The elk appeared, standing proudly over us. We cowered under its soulless gaze as the others taunted us with their constant yipping. With one puff of the elk's lungs, a green fume escaped from its nostrils and into the air. It clouded around us, taking up every last inch of breathable oxygen. I watched Asher drop to the ground first, then Charli. I waved my hands in front of my face and tried to hold my breath for as long as possible, but eventually, I gave in. I inhaled and once more, everything went dark.

~ 26 ~

TUCKER

Incognizant of what had just happened, I woke up with immense pain in the back of my skull, stretching all the way down through my spine. My eyes opened sluggishly but failed to actually show me any of my surroundings. It felt like there was a cloud of smoke covering them. I blinked rapidly, trying to clear up my vision. When I finally did so, I had wished the smoky blindness would return. Straight in front of me was the pure darkness of the forest. I could only faintly make out the outline of a few trees. I glanced down to see a rope tied around me, and when I followed the length of the rope with my eyes, I realized it was tied around my friends as well. We were all sitting shoulder-to-shoulder, spread around the trunk of a tree, the maple tree. Above us, were the old-fashioned lanterns that I had hung all around the property for Shiloh. Their flames were oddly still within their glass casing. Mounted among the lanterns were those wretched gargoyles. They gazed down upon me, grinning those wicked grins.

I shimmied around, trying to get the others to wake up. Charli was on my right and Luke was to the left of me. I could barely see the others sitting farther down the line. I tapped Charli with my foot over and over again until her eyelids finally fluttered open. She had a much more panicked reaction than I did when she realized she couldn't see after first waking up.

"Oh no," she heaved, squirming around in the dirt. "No, no-"

"Charli, calm down. I'm right here," I tried to reassure her, tapping her with my foot again.

Staring blindly, she paused. "Tuck?" She reached her hand desperately in the direction of my voice.

"It's me. I'm here," I said, barely touching her fingertips with my own.

I saw a temporary wave of relief hit Charli. She placed her head roughly against the bark of the tree and tilted her chin up as if trying to look at the sky.

"Tucker, I can't see anything. Why can't I see?" Her voice grew shaky once more and she began to kick in the dirt with her legs.

"Just give it a minute," I spoke up quickly, "Keep blinking."

Her eyelids opened and shut rampantly, and then slowly, she began to see our surroundings as well. The second she noticed the rope, she lost it. "What the hell?" she said loudly. She strained every tired muscle in her body to break loose, but it was no use. "Let us go, you freaks!" Even her voice sounded worn out as she screamed.

"Charli! Charli, stop!" I yelled over her.

She looked at me with a frightened expression. It was one of the only times I had seen true fear in her.

"Just calm down for a second. Please," I huffed, my breath showing in the frigid air. I maintained steady eye contact with her as she got her breathing to slow. "Charli, look where we are. We're at the same tree I woke up at the first time. She brought us back."

Charli took in the whole situation, looking around wide-eyed. "She brought us back for a reason," she stared at the lanterns, "But what is that reason? Is this some sort of séance?"

"Well done, darling," that unmistakable voice called out. Shiloh's green eyes appeared dead ahead of us. Her ashen figure became visible in the fiery light as she approached. Alongside her stood Holt, silent but smirking. "You've found yourself quite an intelligent friend, Mr. Romero. If only you picked up on the signs as quickly as she did," the woman sighed.

"What do you want with us, Shiloh?" I demanded.

She gave me a quizzical look. "Shiloh? Who is she?" The woman squinted at me with a sly smirk.

Both Charli and I reacted with the same confused look, not knowing what to say.

"Ah, yes, you've just reminded me. *Shiloh*," she said, her smirk turning into a maniacal grin. She kept her hands clasped together as she walked gracefully towards us. "Shiloh Farrington: the girl who grew up here with her Halloween-obsessed family, the girl who was oh-so heartbroken when those parents of hers each died suddenly in the night . . . the girl whose body still roams this very property. You thought *I* was her?"

"What do you mean? If you're not Shiloh . . . then who are you?" I questioned.

"I believe your friend may have a clue as to who I am?" Shiloh glanced at Charli beside me.

Charli furrowed her brow with all the same confusion as before. "What? Are you some psychotic, female serial killer?" She put every ounce of her attitude into that answer.

Shiloh adjusted her gaze as if pushing Charli to say something she already knew. It was as if the two shared a connection for a brief moment and Shiloh transferred the information from her brain to Charli's.

Charli shifted uncomfortably. "Or are you a witch?" she asked hesitantly.

"A witch?" Shiloh chuckled. "Now, dear, that's just insulting. There is no one particular name for my being. A witch, the true ones, are limited to their curses and their potions and their mindless card readings. But *I*, I serve a much higher purpose than that. Within these woods, I control the very air that runs through your lungs. I am the trees and the earth and the wind. All these things are mine and mine alone. Your God has no place here."

"So what's your real name then?" Charli interrogated with a nod of her head.

Just then, a puff of smoke appeared from the woman's hand, and in it, was a piece of paper. She bent down and placed it in my lap. "Anthony so desperately wanted to give this to you, but seeing that he's no longer with us . .

. well . . . I suppose I should be the one to deliver it," she uttered.

Scribbled on the paper, almost illegible, was a name. "Metsah," I spoke quietly. The words stung my lips like a blade.

Suddenly, the others started to wake up. One by one they screamed as they felt the utter terror fill their minds. I felt the rope getting tugged in every direction as they all fidgeted around. The woman cackled maliciously, taking enjoyment from seeing us struggle. As she laughed, there was a sudden uproar of howls and screeches from throughout the forest, and in a matter of seconds, they began to close in, circling the tree.

All at once, her creatures appeared. First, was one I recognized immediately: the stage clown. From the trees, crawled out the goblins we had previously seen. They were even more hideous in the light with their upturned noses and long snake-like tongues. Then, there were the creatures that broke themselves directly from the trees. Their skin was bark and they had no mouths, but their eyes lit up like lanterns. There was a frail hag with wrinkled skin and eyes as black as night. Her hair was raggedy and thin just like the tattered dress she wore. There was a couple dressed up in old, bloodstained, Victorian clothes from the shoulders down, but their heads were covered in the most disturbing masks. The closer they got, I realized the masks were not just masks at all, but real-life animal heads; one was a rabbit and the other a fox. There were giant creatures made up of tangled vines that carried jack-o-lanterns for heads. Their gangly arms hung far lower than their waists. There were terrible monsters that hopped on the ground with hooven feet. They had human arms that had been distorted and twisted into a freakish version of wings that hung at their sides, which left their torsos to be the only human thing about them. Their heads were the worst part; they had heads like birds, except their beaks were stretched too far out. These monsters let out horrendous screeches like they held a dying human inside of them; it was a sound I'll never forget. My least favorite was the gigantic half-spider that lowered itself down from somewhere up above. I remembered that one from the barn. The other half of this creature was a woman. Her regular arms were just as long and spindly as the eight legs beneath her. She looked at me cruelly with six, pitch-black eyes on her face. And lastly, were the bats. No, of course these couldn't be normal bats. They were humongous, pale beasts that really looked more like vampires than actual bats. They had beady eyes, their skin was covered in patchy fur, and their ears were almost as big as the goblins'. They cried out in unison above us as they flooded in.

My friends screamed louder and louder at every monstrous face they saw. The creatures were taking great pleasure in all of the fear. They crawled around in the dirt and grinned terrifying grins at each person. Jolene and Abbie got it the worst. Their cries rang out so loudly that you might've thought they were getting murdered right then and there. Being closest to Luke, I could hear his whimpers line up with Austin's. And even Asher, as tough as he was, could be heard begging for mercy.

As I looked at all the beasts, I realized there were at least two missing, which only meant that someone else was somewhere in the woods getting terrorized as well. That's when I caught Metsah staring right through me.

"I see exactly what you are thinking, but there's no need to worry, they'll be back soon enough. Ah, and they've brought you a gift. Consider it a token of our affection," she grinned widely. Her smile was no longer perfect, instead her teeth were gray and sharp like broken stones.

"We don't want your gift," I growled. I hoped she could see the disgust on my face.

"Oh, but I think you'll find it quite amusing." Her grin wore off into a snarl.

"I have a better idea," Charli's surly voice interrupted. "How about you tell us what the hell these things are," she looked around at the monsters, "Or better yet, you can tell us what *you* are."

Metsah's patience was clearly running thin with Charli. She had always made it very clear that she hated disrespect, or maybe it was just disobedience she hated. Her lips formed a thin scowl when she looked at Charli. "I suppose there's time for a little story," the woman said through gritted teeth.

The monsters gathered closer to her, temporarily giving the others on the opposite side of the tree some peace. I saw all their ugly faces line up in front of me like it was storytime with Metsah.

"Shall we start from the beginning?" Metsah glanced at one of the giant pumpkin creatures next to her. As she grinned, it grinned; its thick, precisely carved mouth moved so unnaturally. "My dear Tucker, much like you, I was horrifically abused as a child. I felt as though there was not a soul left to care for me."

Suddenly, a vivid image popped into my head, almost like a dream, but I was still fully awake. I saw the face of a little girl, scarred and bruised. Her hair was dark and raggedy, and the sickly pale skin of her face was sunken.

"But I learned that there was *one* being left who did care. He gave me these powers. He filled me with the everlasting pain and sorrow that those cruel people deserved to feel," Metsah continued. Her tone became more passionately angry as she went on.

I then saw the horrific plague that the little girl had sent upon her people. It spread over them like wildfire, infesting their bodies and twisting them into hideous, malnourished shadows of who they once were. Children lay dead in their mothers' arms and people weeped like I had never seen before. I shook my head, trying to get rid of the image, but I couldn't stop it.

"I saved them the time before their great suffering in the eternal flames," Metsah hissed.

"You poisoned them!" I shouted furiously. My eyes locked onto Metsah's, watching the fury rise. "You murdered them all! You took the lives of innocent children for the wrongs of their parents!" I could feel the spit emulating from my mouth as I shouted in rage.

Charli only gazed at me with the utmost sympathy. She knew it was finally time for me to battle face-to-face with the Devil.

"Given your situation, you have felt the same fire burn within you, Tucker! You know the overwhelming urge to take the lives of your abusers. You have heard his whispers crying out to you, telling you to do something about it. All you had to do was answer. He could have given you so much," the woman fought back.

"Clearly, God told me to fight those urges because they can't possibly do any good!"

Metsah became suddenly still and her voice calm. "Look what good your God has done. If He truly cared, why does He make you suffer so?" The vacant expression in her eyes was terrifying.

"Tucker," Charli voiced quietly, leaning closer to me. "She's just trying to mess with your head."

I knew Charli was trying to help, but I ignored her. For once, I wanted to use my curiosity to help me. "I want to hear the rest of your story. How did you get to Shiloh?" I asked intently.

Metsah smirked. "When she first came to me, I saw how distraught she was. I *felt* it. Just like you and I, she sought relief from her home. So I gave it to her. I freed her from their grasp."

The images began to reappear. This time, there was a different face. She looked a lot like the other little girl, but everything about her was softer, kinder. I watched her walk through the forest naively as the trees whispered to each other. Then, in a flash, the girl's eyes were no longer her own. Metsah's green eyes took their place and blinked right at me as if I was standing there with her. I saw the plant she used to kill the girl's mother and the gory death of her father. They were both helpless in their endeavors but there was nothing to prevent it.

Metsah observed me in a concentrated manner as I saw her visions. But it seemed they weren't just visions, they were her memories. Her *unreliable* memories.

"You didn't help that girl. You stole her. Metsah, all you did was take her life and use it to do your own bidding."

"I got rid of the people who tormented her! I saved her!" Metsah exclaimed.

"No. You took something so precious from her that she will never get back. You didn't even give the poor girl a choice. *You* had a choice and you screwed it up big time," I explained.

Even through all the cracks and crevices of her ashen skin, Metsah's scowl was still visible. Her and I locked gazes, and I saw all the things that could have been and all that was not. Accepting one offer from her would have taken away every bit of happiness that was left for me. I was just glad that God had fought so hard to protect me.

The uncomfortable silence that had fallen over us quickly faded away when her monsters let out simultaneous howls. Metsah's eyes broke away and her hideous grin returned as she peered into the distance. She turned around and disappeared into the dark.

"Tucker," Charli whispered, shoving me from the side.

"What?"

"I don't have my phone. Do you have yours?" she asked, searching her pockets.

Me, being stupid, looked at her in confusion. "Why are

you worried about our phones right now? I think we've got bigger issues," I said.

She whipped her head towards me, glaring. "Oh, I don't know, Tucker. Maybe so that we can call for help!" she scolded.

"Right. Right," I nodded quickly, searching my pockets as well. My eyes scoured the ground in a hope that the phones might have just fallen in the dirt, but no luck.

Just then, Metsah's dark figure returned from the shadows. She kept her hands tucked secretly behind her back as she approached. She was very careful with her steps, walking toe to heel as if not to disturb the ground. Alongside her, appeared the two missing beasts. The gigantic, sickly elk, and the very first monster I had ever seen in the forest: the werewolf.

"Thank you, Deimos," Metsah looked at the elk, "And thank you, Keres," she turned to the werewolf.

"Oh, good. They have names," Charli muttered sarcastically.

"Oh, no," I mumbled to myself as I realized what was probably in her hands.

"Aren't you so glad, Mr. Romero? Your friends have returned, and as I promised," she brought her hands out from behind her, "They have brought you a gift."

Those of us facing her directly were the first to gasp, while the others strained their heads around the trunk of the tree to get a glimpse. Once Abbie saw it, she let out a blood-curdling scream.

"What the fuck?" Luke gasped, mouth agape.

Charli shut her eyes tight and turned her head the

other way, holding back tears. As they all tried to look away from the grim sight, my eyes were helplessly stuck, petrified like I had just seen Medusa.

In the palms of Metsah, was a human head. Lydia's head. Her jaw was hanging and blood streamed from her eyes. Although it was hard to see, there was also dried blood caked into her brown hair, which was so knotted that it looked like it had been dragged through a hedge.

"Aw, what's wrong? You don't like it?" Metsah taunted menacingly, waving Lydia's head around by a section of her hair.

"Oh my God. Oh my God!" Abbie screamed from the other side of the tree.

The monsters roared in an upheaval as they fed on our distressed energy.

"What is it?" Asher shouted over the distraught cries. He was on the direct opposite side, so there was no physical way for him to see.

"Don't! Don't look! She has a fucking head!" Austin yelled at him.

"What?" I heard Asher shout again.

Austin thrashed about, trying to break loose. "She's holding a human head!"

Metsah tossed Lydia's head at my feet and cackled. Her amusement only brought the creatures more joy. They jumped around, clapping and dancing, flinging their limbs around wildly.

Charli squinted reluctantly back at Metsah. "What is wrong with you? Demented freak!"

As the distracted monsters pranced blindly, there was

a sudden tug on the rope. Charli and I glanced down, watching the rope press into our skin. I reached my head as far as I could to see what was going on from the other side when surprisingly, the rope fell in my lap. Charli and I gave each other the same baffled expression. Then, we saw Austin scrambling to stand up with a pocket knife in hand. He hit his head on the base of a lantern and knocked right from its place. It fell to the ground near some of the creatures and burst into flames. The beasts all recoiled back, screeching in pain. Austin kicked the broken lantern closer to them and booked it into the darkness. As the flames reached for the monsters, all of them, even those far away from it, cried out. Metsah buckled to the ground, holding a hand over her chest.

Charli and I exchanged a quick wide-eyed look and both said the same thing. "Fire." We leaped up from the ground, shoving the rope off of us, and snatched the lanterns from the tree. We threw them in the direction of the different creatures and let the flames slowly catch on the ground. Many of the beasts ran and the ones that stayed cowered in immense pain as if their bones were crumbling within them even though the flames had not yet touched their skin.

"Run!" I shouted to the others over the desperate cries.

With the adrenaline pumping once more, we ran from the tree, except for Charli. Asher and I looked back to see her navigating her way through the crippled monsters.

"Charli! What are you doing? Let's go!" I yelled, backtracking to her.

She ignored my pleas and knelt down next to Holt. I

squinted through the rising flames and watched her aim something in Metsah's direction. There was a sudden blast of noise and then silence from all the beasts, including Metsah. I realized what Charli had done as she tucked a pistol in the back of her belt.

"Okay, now we can go," she huffed casually, grabbing our arms and running. It seemed her toughness had returned to her.

~ 27 ~

TUCKER

With the rest of the group nowhere in sight, Asher, Charli, and I rushed through the forest aimlessly. We kept the talking to a minimum just in case there were still monsters around to pick up on our voices. The silence was almost worse than listening to the cries of Metsah's creatures.

Stupidly, we thought that shooting Metsah had worked because eventually, we came to an opening past the trees where the front lights were visible. We really believed that her tricks were done for and that we would be able to escape. As soon as I saw that open space, all I could think about was going to sleep. Metsah's mental torment had left my head beyond tired.

"It actually worked," Asher said with a relieved sigh as we crossed over that dividing line.

The alleviation in us only lasted moments. We were just a few steps out of the trees when those frightening howls started back up, making us all stop in our tracks.

"You just had to jinx it," Charli voiced, squeezing her eyes shut.

Almost coincidentally, thick clouds swept over the moon, blocking out its light, and suddenly, it felt like we were right back in that God-forsaken forest. With nowhere else to go, we ran up the hill until we found a concession stand to take cover behind.

"They're alive. That means she's alive too," I said calmly. I glanced over my shoulder at the woods. It waited ominously for our return. When I turned back to my friends, I could see that the worry was getting to them again.

"So then how the hell do we kill all of them?" Asher questioned. He kicked his foot in the dirt in a stressed manner.

"The fire," I said, looking directly at Charli. "The fire was working. It just wasn't strong enough. If we light the whole place up then it should get to Metsah too. If we take out the source, we take them all out."

Charli crossed her arms. "Listen, I know this is like life or death right now, but if we're successful and we burn the whole place to the ground we're gonna get arrested for arson. I mean think about it. People are gonna see the fire from miles away."

"Then we just won't get caught," Asher spoke up. Even though we were literally on death row at that very moment, there was excitement in his eyes about getting to burn it all down. There was even a contagious little grin forming at the corner of his mouth.

"Well, unless either of you two have matches in your

pockets, I don't see how we're gonna do this," Charli pointed out, dropping her arms to her sides.

"The barn probably has something. That place is filled with random tools. Who knows? Maybe with the insanity that goes on in this place, we'll find a flamethrower in there," I said. Although it was crazy, part of me really did hope to find something like that in the barn. We needed a miracle.

We checked and double-checked and triple-checked to make sure there were no more of Metsah's freaks hanging around before we left our hiding spot. Nobody seemed to be walking around and from what we could tell, the stands were empty. No monsters, and no customers either (that part was also concerning). I hoped that the people were able to leave the property before coming to any harm. But unfortunately, I knew that if any of them had been taken, Metsah would have already killed them in her rage of searching for my friends and I.

The three of us booked it across the property, our eyes focused solely on the barn. I led them to the side of the building in search of the door I had previously used to get in there. I guess Metsah had grown suspicious of me after that little incident because when I went back to push it open, the thing wouldn't budge an inch.

"You've got to be kidding me," I mumbled to myself as I forced all my weight against the door.

Asher and Charli kept a tense lookout as they waited for me.

"Any day now, Tuck," Charli grumbled, her eyes fully alert.

I rammed my shoulder into the door again and again. "The dang thing won't open," I said, finally giving up with a heavy sigh.

"Well, we can't go through the front. It'll be way too obvious," Charli voiced impatiently.

"Move," Asher suddenly spoke. He hoisted a rusted shovel from the collection of junky, old tools on the ground.

"She is *definitely* going to hear this," Charli said, putting her hands on her head in a stressed manner.

"Do you want to have a chance at getting rid of her or not?" Asher questioned rhetorically.

Charli backed away from the door with an apprehensive look. "Just know that if Metsah wants to brutally maim the person who broke down her door, I'm telling her it was you," she teased.

Asher rolled his eyes and with one strong heave, the shovel went right through the wooden door. Chunks of wood could be heard hitting the floor inside. He continued until he broke away enough of the door so that we could sneak in.

Charli knelt down and peered through the hole. "Crap. I can't see a thing in there."

"Ladies first," Asher joked, placing the shovel quietly back on the ground.

"Fine, wimp," Charli mocked. She crept towards the low opening and looked in hesitantly.

"Wait," I stopped her, "Mestah could still have her other monsters in there."

The two of them looked at me in bewilderment.

"I thought she brought all of them out for tonight. You know, for her murder show," Charli said bluntly.

"I thought so too, but last time I was here, she had a bunch of unfinished ones just sitting in here. And at least one of them was definitely awake. I don't know about the others," I explained.

Charli looked up at Asher for a brief moment with a mixture of disappointment and irritation. He just shrugged. Then, Charli looked at me with a devious smile. I could tell that was her "oh well" face.

"Too late now," she stuck her hands inside the jagged opening, "Go big or go home." With little effort, she got herself quickly into the barn.

Asher and I stood timidly outside, waiting for her to say something. After a long period of time in complete silence, I knelt down to try and see where she had gone. All of a sudden, her face appeared in the darkness. Surprised, I lost balance and fell back into the dirt.

"Would you two get your asses in here already? We don't have time for this shy shit," Charli whispered harshly. We could tell she was getting more on edge because the swearing was starting to come back out. Her face disappeared once more inside the structure.

"Come on," Asher said, helping me up. He ushered me through the door and took one last glance around before squeezing himself through too. It was much more difficult for him to fit considering his brawny build.

Charli pointed at him demeaningly and let out a hushed laugh as we watched him struggle to get through.

"Shut up," Asher scowled, contorting his body in funny ways to not hit the jagged edges of wood.

Once we were all inside, I felt around the frame of the door for whatever had been keeping it shut. As I ran my hand above the handle, I felt multiple sliding locks. They were placed all the way up to the top of the door, counting five in total. "A little overkill," I mumbled, unlocking each one. When I yanked the door open, the resistance nearly broke the rickety handle clean-off. A shred of moonlight poured into the structure, giving us back a little bit of our vision. Along with the needed light, was a puff of some not-so-needed dust that fell off the top of the door as if it hadn't been opened since the last time Metsah locked it shut.

"Hey, Tuck," Asher whispered, tapping me on the shoulder.

"What?" I spun around to see what they were both seeing.

"This is what you were talking about, isn't it?" he murmured, staring at the faces of all Metsah's unfinished creations.

Charli looked on in astonishment at the rows of horrific figures. It was like an army of the dead, but for all we knew, they could have just as easily become the *undead*.

"Let's find what we need and get out of here quickly," I told them, starting up the stairs. As I looked at the bottom step, I realized there were indents in the wood. They were round and at the tips of each curve were scratch marks, excuse me, *claw* marks. I followed the imprints all the way up the staircase until they disappeared into the shadows.

"Go with him. I'll keep watch down here," Asher told Charli.

She nodded and followed up after me, keeping one hand on the rail at all times. I saw her catch a glimpse of the marks on the stairs just like I had but she chose to ignore them and hurry up to the top.

There was hardly any light reaching that upper level and in the farthest corner of the area, there was no light at all. Charli and I quietly went through each item we could see, those outside the boxes and those inside the boxes. I kept a close eye on Asher at the bottom of the staircase to make sure he was still there and still breathing. Every time I looked, he had one hand plastered to the stair railing and one hand dug tensely into his side as he stared down the unfinished props.

"I'm sorry about Lydia by the way," Charli voiced from a couple feet away. "I know you were closer with her than I ever was." She pretended to intensely look at certain items she found to make up for the awkwardness of the conversation, never looking directly at me.

I glanced up at her from the bin I had been searching through, surprised by her sudden empathy. It was rare that any of us ever got to hear from Charli's soft side because she just wasn't like that. If something ever went wrong in her life she would just make a joke out of it and move on before anyone had time to say anything. At that moment, I was given the time, but I had no idea what to say.

Charli went on, rummaging through the boxes in silence.

"If anything, I'm the one who should be sorry. I dragged you all into this mess," I finally spoke. "I'm basically the one who killed her. It's my fault."

"That was not your fault, Tuck." She glared at me, but not in the truly angry sort of way, more like she was mad that I had just said something stupid. "That woman — if you can even call her that — is pure evil. She's murdered countless people, and Lydia just happened to be the one tonight."

I shook my head. "Metsah targeted her because she knew Lydia was connected to me," I huffed, teary-eyed. "Just like the rest of them. Just like you two," I peered down at Asher. "And now, you guys are permanently in danger."

Charli dropped the things in her hands and knelt down next to me. The comfort I could feel radiating off of her only made me want to cry even more.

I stared back at her and couldn't help but think of one person. "Charli, I already lost one sibling. I'm not going to lose another."

As if all the built-up pain that had been plaguing me for so many years suddenly transferred over to her, she wrapped her arms tightly around me. "We're not going anywhere, Tuck."

The healing moment was suddenly broken by Asher's nervous voice. "Hey, uh, have you guys found anything yet? I can hear those creatures outside getting louder," he called out.

Just then, Charli's eyes locked onto something behind me. Moving past me, she crawled toward the total darkness in the corner. I swiveled around on the floor to see her hovering her hand over something. It was another hand. But whose was it? I followed Charli hesitantly, not knowing what to really expect. Based on how the shadows covered it, the hand looked like it could have been dismembered, but when Charli tugged on it, the resistance told us it was still intact to the rest of the body. We grabbed hold of the arm and dragged it from the darkness. I was horrified to see Anthony's pale face staring up at me.

~ 28 ~

TUCKER

I couldn't take my eyes off the battered corpse at my feet. There were giant claw marks dug into Anthony's torso and face. The slashes were so deep that they distorted his facial features, but I knew it was him immediately by his grungy clothes and the stench of cigarette smoke that was burned into them. That was it. The cigarettes. Anthony smoked so much that he always carried a lighter on him. I didn't hesitate to start digging through each one of his pockets.

"What are you doing?" Charli questioned, staring at my rampant searching.

I pulled Anthony's lighter from the chest pocket of his shirt. "Bingo," I said, holding it up for her to see. I tested it once to see if the old thing even worked anymore. It did. "I found our fire," I grinned, "Let's go. We don't have much time."

Forgetting to remain quiet, we rushed down the stairs, our feet hitting each step louder than the time before.

Asher was startled by the sudden noise and leaped back when he saw us coming.

"Did you find something that will work?" he asked.

I held up the lighter, and with impeccable timing, a pair of eyes lit up from the darkness behind him. We had woken the dead. I blinked a few times to check if I was actually seeing the eyes, but then, they began to blink back, their amber glow getting brighter and brighter.

"Crap! They're awake!" I exclaimed.

Asher and Charli turned to see what I was seeing. We didn't waste a second in running out of that side door.

"Go! Go!" I said in a violent whisper, waving for them to move in any direction other than the barn.

Being the closest thing to us, we took cover in the outskirts of the trees. I figured it wasn't dense enough there to really count as part of the forest, so maybe we would be safe. We ducked behind the largest tree we could find and crouched on the ground.

"Now she knows where we are," Charli voiced frantically, peeking out at the barn.

I shook my head. "We're on her property. She always knew where we were. Like Mr. Morales said, this woman has eyes everywhere."

"Then why didn't she have that thing in there just kill us?" Charli tilted her head to the side.

"Because she's waiting for us to go back into the woods. I'd be willing to bet that's where she's the strongest," I explained.

The howls and cries from the forest rang out loudly as if the beasts heard me and were agreeing.

"But we have to go back in there anyway? So what are we gonna do?" Asher spoke.

I sat in deep contemplation. I tried to think of all the things I knew about Metsah and her little freaks. I had a hunch that she would make the experience as miserable as possible for all of us with her sadistic personality. "Metsah seems like she enjoys playing with her prey before she catches it. She won't kill us immediately. She'll wait for the drama and suspense to really kick in, and then it will be some creative murder. If I had to guess, she's probably going to use her monsters to keep us in line. So . . . we have to keep her monsters busy. We'll utilize the fire to keep them away from us. And then-"

"We light the whole place up," Charli smirked.

I looked at her and nodded, "We light it up."

As we wandered back into the thicker part of the trees, there was no way of knowing where Metsah's creatures were. The trees hid them like perfect camouflage. There were moments when I envisioned the eyes of one of them staring at me from afar, but all I had to do was look again and they were gone. I felt like I was going insane. Metsah's mind games were getting to me and I could only imagine how they were affecting the others. Many times, I thought about Luke, Austin, Jolene, and Abbie. I wondered if they were even still alive because we hadn't seen any of them since previously escaping the woods. Knowing Abbie had her limp and Jolene had to practically carry her, I wasn't too hopeful. As for the boys, they weren't the brightest of the bunch, so catching them should have been a piece of cake for the monsters. The way the moon poked out from beyond the tops of the trees gave me slight hope. It felt as though God was guiding us with the single beam of light that illuminated from it.

"We need to find the maple tree again. That's the core of Metsah's power," I told them.

We kept our heads low and our voices lower. It seemed to keep us at least partially hidden from Metsah's sight unless she really was just luring us in the whole time.

After some time, Charli grabbed Asher and I, stopping us. "There," she whispered, pointing in the distance.

From afar, I caught a glimpse of the shimmering red leaves of the maple tree. The area surrounding it appeared to be vacant, almost as if nothing had ever happened.

Asher and I both started toward the tree, but we were suddenly yanked back by Charli.

"Wait," she gripped our arms tightly, "This is too easy."

"What do you mean? The tree is right there. Let's go," Asher argued, pulling away.

As he wandered towards the blood-red target, Charli and I noticed something in unison. Charli leaped at Asher and threw her arms around him. At that same moment, the werewolf, Keres, dropped down from one of the trees up above and landed only inches away from them. Charli dragged Asher back as if to shield him. The creature stood on her hind legs, towering over us. Her eyes were somehow a deeper red than the leaves of the maple tree, and yet they also glowed brighter. We could hear the beast's breathing grow more intense as it gradually prowled closer to us.

"Told you it was too fucking easy," Charli remarked as

she and Asher continued to take steps back. Their eyes never broke from Keres'. "Hey, Tuck," Charli voiced as calmly as possible. Her hand clenched tighter into Asher's arm. "I think now would be a good time to get a fire going."

I stood my ground and remained steady as the beast got within five feet of us. I waited until Charli and Asher were fully behind me to flick on the lighter. With one swipe of my arm, I lit the brush in front of me. The flames caught quickly, creating a wide dividing line between us and Keres. The werewolf cried out when it saw the fire and stumbled backward. Now being the one shielding both of them, I kept the lighter aflame and used it like a knight would a sword, guarding us from the monster. Unfortunately, Keres began to see that the flame was not growing unmanageably in height and she regained that fearsome look in her eyes. Her front paws hit the ground and she took a giant leap over the flames.

"Go!" Charli screamed, shoving us to the side.

We darted through the nearby trees and past the fire, barely escaping the bite of Keres' teeth. I tried to light various bushes and branches that were within my reach as we went, giving us a few extra seconds. Charli tried to guide us in the direction of the maple tree, but that werewolf caused us to make so many sudden twists and turns that we eventually lost sight of the tree altogether. Along with the chase, the flames finally began to grow. We couldn't see anything past them at a certain point, so it was like running blind.

After stumbling through all the smoke for a while, we

found ourselves on the opposite side of a wall made up solely of fire. On the other side, stood a wrathful Keres. She made multiple attempts at climbing up the trees, but the fire stretched all the way up those as well. The beast howled in frustration as she paced back and forth along the wall.

"Now, why did you have to go and make this all so complicated?" a familiar voice called out from nearby.

The three of us spun around at the exact same time, our eyes searching everywhere.

"You have caused my children so much distress," the woman's voice echoed. Her figure was nowhere to be seen.

"Where the hell is she?" Asher muttered as we rotated in a circle, back to back.

"I don't like this," Charli muttered.

Just then, the figure of Deimos, the giant elk, took its place on our side of the fire, only a couple yards away. He emerged like a shadowy mist from the trees, and upon him, was Metsah; he was her graceful steed.

"Did you really think you could get rid of me that easily? A bullet? Come on, girl," she directed her voice towards Charli, "I thought you were smarter than that." She smirked arrogantly. The flames reflected in her snake-like eyes, perfectly creating an image to the gates of Hell. "You cannot kill *me*. I will always return, just as my Lord has promised," Metsah hissed.

As Deimos shifted in his steps, a flash of red showed up from behind him, far behind him. The tree.

"Your 'Lord' is a fake, lady," Charli spoke up. I wasn't so sure how long Charli's taunts would hold up when Metsah was dragging us all to our deaths, but then I realized it was all to help give us some time. Charli nudged my back to tell me she had seen the tree as well.

"You're growing weak, aren't you, Metsah?" I said loudly. As I spoke, I could hear Charli telling Asher to get ready to run. "The fire is hurting you. That's why you ride upon that beast."

The heat of the flames was creeping closer, which only forced us towards Metsah more.

Metsah tilted her head as if to challenge what I had said. "Would you like to see just how powerful I can be?" she spoke with a disturbingly calm tone. With careful movements, she lowered herself off of the monstrous elk and onto the ground. The way Deimos stood behind Metsah gave the impression that his antlers were actually a part of her, making her truly look like an embodiment of the Devil. In the distance, we could see that the maple tree was altering in shape. It twisted and groaned until the center of its trunk began to form a red, fiery pit. It looked like a portal to Hell, and that portal was giving Metsah power. In all the cracks of her ashen skin, that same red glow radiated, giving her the appearance of being made from molten lava.

"Tucker," Asher whispered in a cautious tone as the woman approached.

I could feel that we were all tensing up with each step she took. My hand gripped the lighter like it was our life-line, and technically, it was. Metsah slithered towards us faster and faster.

"Tucker!" Charli shouted suddenly.

That was when we broke apart and began to run. I tried to follow Asher but I was stopped by a sudden blast of dirt from in front of me. A tree root shot up from the ground and wrapped tightly around my wrist, yanking me backward. The root squeezed tighter and tighter, trying to force me to let go of the lighter. Being the only one in my line of vision, I yelled for Asher's help. He spun around and gained a horrified look on his face.

"Here! Take it!" I shouted to him, raising the lighter in the air with my free hand. Just as the object left my fingertips, a second root sprawled up that wrist and dragged me into the dirt. I fell to my knees and watched the lighter land only inches away from Asher's feet. When he knelt down to pick it up, I noticed Metsah out of the corner of my eye. She raised her hand and simultaneously another tree root moved with it. "Asher!" I exclaimed immediately. But my warning was too late. The root swiped his legs right out from under him and he tumbled into the dirt. The lighter was nowhere in sight.

The roots around my wrists started to cut into my arms; the feeling of warm blood dripped down to my fingertips. I writhed in pain as those wretched things continued to force me lower onto the ground. Through my furrowed brow, I could see the roots beginning to fully wrap around Asher. They took over his arms and legs first, then spread over his torso, keeping him completely flattened to the ground. I tried to twist my head back and look for Charli, but between the mix of fire and flying roots, I was practically blind to anything behind me.

Metsah swung her arms from left to right, ensnaring

us in her trap more and more. Her eyes were glowing vibrantly with each motion, but when the flames grew closer, that vibrance would dim temporarily. It was clearly hurting her, just not enough.

All of sudden, a yelp sounded from behind me. The sound distracted Metsah enough for me to turn my head and catch a quick glimpse of Charli. She was standing by the spreading wall of fire with a dead branch in one of her hands, while the other covered a spot on her arm. She was slightly hunched over and was trying to get the branch to light. I took a second, shorter glance and barely saw one of Keres' large black paws swiping at Charli through the fire.

In a matter of seconds, Metsah was able to return her focus to Asher and I, strengthening the power of the tree roots to kill us quicker. I could feel my bones weakening as my arms got pulled farther outward. Through the newly framed tears in my eyes, I could see one of the roots starting to suffocate Asher. It tied itself around his neck and squeezed, causing his face to turn a deep red.

Just as I tried to scream for Charli, I found my neck ensnared by one of the roots as well. It appeared from out of nowhere and sprung at me. At first, the power of it just touching my skin felt like I had been shot with a bullet, but then that pain turned into the cut of a knife. I squeezed my eyes shut, fully expecting my head to pop right off of my body. If that didn't kill me, I was sure that the fire would. I could feel its heat growing closer, and there was nowhere for me to go.

"You pathetic children," Metsah voiced through gritted teeth, "I told you, you cannot get rid of me!"

As her rage grew, so did the intensity of the pain. My blood dripped onto the ground, staining everything it touched. But then, distracted but what I was seeing, my mind put it all on pause.

Out of the corner of my eye, an orange flame appeared in the distance, illuminating a farther part of the woods. It traveled quickly towards the big red maple tree, the flames quivering in the air. Attached to the flames was a hand, Charli's hand. She never looked back as she ran, knowing it was her only chance. I saw Metsah turn her whole body towards the sight in a panic. She held the roots on Asher and I down with a single hand and used her other one to bend the very trunks of trees. Evil faces formed in them with gnashing teeth and scowling eyes. They reached their branches towards Charli like actual hands, desperately grabbing at her and the fire she held. She moved even faster with each seizing branch, dodging their wooden claws. Metsah grabbed onto an antler and Deimos lifted her up. The beast leaped through the trees toward Charli at a faster pace than we had ever seen. The trunks of the trees curved perfectly for him to fit through like a tunnel. Just as Charli got within a couple of yards of the tree, a root snatched her footing. As if it were all in slow motion, I watched her begin to fall to the ground, but as she fell, her arm lifted up with the strength of God, and she threw the torch into the open center of the tree. It swallowed it up without hesitation. In seconds, the flames spread up the bark and engulfed the entire tree.

Mid-leap, Deimos flattened to the ground, his hooves sliding through the dirt. Although trying desperately to hold on, Metsah's body was flung from her steed, and she fell like an angel being thrown out of Heaven. As her body went limp, so did the roots. They released their grasp from Asher and I, and slunk back into the earth beneath. I crumbled to my hands and knees, gasping for air. Asher remained lying on the ground momentarily as his chest heaved. All around us, we could hear the pained cries of Metsah's creatures.

My legs trembled uncontrollably as I attempted to stand. I was no longer worried about the blood that ran down my wrists or the ring around my neck. Instead, I watched anxiously through all of the smoke as Metsah struggled in the distance. She kept trying to get up, but each time, a wave of pain would strike her and she would crumble once more. I ran to Asher and helped him to his feet. No words were needed to communicate that we needed to get out of there as soon as possible. With his arm around my shoulder, we limped in the direction of the burning maple tree. With the wind blowing so strongly, the movement of flames and leaves made it difficult to actually get a clear view of where she was. But once we neared the tree, I saw Charli's body lying close by. I dropped to my knees next to her and felt her arm for a heartbeat. It was there but it was dim. She must have gone unconscious when she was knocked down by the root.

"Is she alright?" Asher coughed. "We have to get her up. The fire's getting out of control." He waved his hand in front of his face as the smoke surrounded us.

Branches could be heard snapping off of trees and hitting the dirt as the fire devoured the entirety of the woods. The air was so polluted that even the stars above could not be seen.

I shook Charli and lightly tapped her face, desperately trying to get her to wake up. Asher and I continuously looked back at Metsah, who appeared to be crawling closer to us even through the torturous pain she was experiencing. Her claw-like hands gripped at the earth and pulled with all the strength left within her.

"I could have saved you!" she bellowed. Her face was full of a sadness I had never seen before. "Why are you doing this to me?" she continued on in a sorrowful voice. Every time she spoke, the fire singed her body in a new and more agonizing way.

I did my best to ignore her pleas and focused my attention on Charli. Eventually, Charli's eyelids fluttered open. She didn't seem to be too hurt besides the claw marks in her arm from Keres and an obvious pain in the side of her head.

"Come on, Charli. We have to go right now," I said, lifting her up.

She was wobbly at first, disoriented from all the smoke. Her eyes, as well as ours, were filling with tears at the pure sting of it.

The three of us wrapped our arms around each other and limped farther and farther from the fire. When one of us would stumble, the others would be there to lift us all back up and push each other to keep going. As we went, the howls of agony continued from behind us, but we refused to look back until we were finally out of that wretched forest.

After nearly coughing our lungs up and losing most of our vision, we made it to a clearing, and in that clearing, stood our abandoned church. It sat there humbly, waiting for our arrival with open arms. We climbed inside through one of the windows and dropped tiredly to the ground. Our bodies ached in every way imaginable but as we sat there, a sense of peace flowed over us all.

When I gained some strength to peer back out the window, I saw the fire completely overtaking the forest. The flames ended perfectly at the edge, never reaching our safe haven. As meek as that structure was, it protected us from the evil outside. While I watched that orange glow illuminate the night, I noticed a figure amidst it all. Metsah lay crumpled on the ground, burning as she once had and as she always would. Her monsters cried in agony as they died alongside their mother. A part of me pitied the horrible sight, but I knew it was just that last trick that Metsah tried to use on me. Pity was powerful. But the truth is, there was no pity to be had at all, not for the Devil.

~ 29 ~

TUCKER

At some point, we all must have fallen asleep in the church from our exhaustion. I was the first to wake up from the painfully obnoxious sound of fire engines. I slid myself out from underneath the pew where I had been sleeping and looked out the window. The sky was still dark and the suffocating stench of smoke permeated every inch of the air. Some of the forest was still burning, but most of it had died out. The trees were all charred to their cores and any grass that had once existed in those woods was erased.

I decided to wake up Asher and Charli so that we could find somewhere to actually breathe fresh air. We climbed out of the rickety building and made our way to the street. As we walked along the darkened road, multiple cop cars raced passed, their sirens blaring.

"I wonder where they're all going," Asher said sarcastically, giving us a tired grin.

"It's about time they actually do their job," Charli

murmured. She watched the vehicles speed by with sunken eyes.

In reality, we all looked and felt like dogshit, as Charli would say. Our hair was disheveled, we were randomly covered in all sorts of bloody marks and bruises, and our faces looked like they hadn't seen sleep in over a week.

"So, what now?" Asher shrugged, pulling his hood over his messy head of hair.

We trudged alongside the road in silence for a minute, feeling totally lost.

"I have an idea," I told them. "I think Mr. Morales will want to hear that his business is gonna start doing better than ever."

The three of us walked all the way up that road to the hill where the bar was. We quietly got past all the cops and firemen who were running around Metsah's property. They didn't even seem to care that three suspicious-looking teenagers were at the scene of the fire.

Luckily, the doors to the bar were still open. Inside, Mr. Morales stood at the window with a bottle in his hand, watching the situation next door. He was so caught up by it that he didn't even look at us when we first walked in. "We're closed. No more drinks tonight-"

"Mr. Morales," I spoke.

We waited solemnly by the doors, not wanting to seem intrusive. He looked at us and his whole expression changed. He didn't seem angry, but he didn't seem happy either. His beard had grown thicker since we had last spoken, and his overall character appeared more tired.

"It was you three," he said quietly. His hand shook

slightly as he lowered the bottle away from his mouth. "You actually got rid of her, didn't you?"

I took a step forward. "We did. And all of her monsters too."

A small, shaky grin formed at the corner of his mouth. "Well, you all look like you've really been to Hell and back," he chuckled. "Come sit down. I'll get you some water." Mr. Morales rushed behind the bar and began fumbling with the glasses. "Sit down. Sit," he urged kindly.

"Hey, uh, you're not gonna tell the police it was us, are you?" Charli asked as we sat down.

Mr. Morales placed the glasses down gently and stared at her gruffly. "Are you kidding? I'm not saying a word to those tools, *except* to tell them that I was right." His expression softened when he saw how relieved we became just by him saying that. "I'm just happy to see that you kids are still alive. There are some other people that I don't think ended up so lucky."

"Did you see a lot of people leave the property before the fire started?" Charli questioned, chugging the water down.

The man paused and leaned his elbows tiredly on the counter. "I can't say. It seemed like a good amount were flooding out of the parking lot at one point, but I'm sure that psycho caught some of them," he shook his head sadly.

In that moment, I couldn't help but feel this overwhelming weight of sadness hit me. I could only imagine all the families that had lost their loved ones that night. I knew what it was like to lose a family member but not to truly *lose* them, to know that there wasn't even the slightest possibility that you would ever see them again.

Mr. Morales picked up on my thoughts pretty quickly. He reached over the counter and placed a hand on my shoulder like a father would. "Look, kid, you did your best. There was only so much three teenagers could do in a situation like that. People were bound to get hurt. Sometimes loss is completely out of our control, and all we can do is mourn that inevitable pain."

I looked into his eyes and saw a person I had only ever wished to meet as a child. He gave me the comfort that neither of my parents ever had. Even though it may have seemed rather insignificant to him I wanted to thank him for that one small moment, but all I could do was smile.

"Besides, Tuck, we really did save a lot of people," Charli nudged me. "He said he saw a lot of them leave," she glanced at Mr. Morales, "And now nobody will have to deal with that woman in the future."

"She's right," Mr. Morales said, refilling our glasses. "You banished that demon back to the fiery pit she crawled out of." He placed his hands on the counter and looked at each of us individually. "Now, you three should go home. Go home and rest. You've been through quite a bit," the man grinned softly.

We finished off the water in our glasses, thanked Mr. Morales for his generosity, and hopped down from the elevated stools.

"Feel free to stop by whenever you have any more ghost stories. And be careful out there. Some crazy people started a big ole' fire," he chuckled, waving to us as we got to the exit.

I paused before walking through the doors. Mr. Morales gave me a final smirk and a prolonged, still wave.

"Thanks again," I voiced before leaving.

The next day, Asher and I were passed out on the couches in his living room. Charli had gone back to her house to make sure her parents knew she was okay. And Asher's parents were unaware that we had even come home because it was so late when we finally snuck back into his house.

My head suddenly shot up when the sound of the doorbell rang throughout all of the rooms downstairs. I rubbed my eyes and checked the clock in Asher's kitchen. We had slept through the entire morning and it was now one o'clock in the afternoon. Then, the doorbell rang again. Asher didn't even move; he was completely passed out. I stumbled off the couch and rubbed my eyes some more. The doorbell rang again.

"Yeah, yeah, hold on," I mumbled, walking towards the front door with my eyes barely open.

The urgency of whoever was on the other side didn't really kick in. I hadn't even thought of the idea that it could be the police waiting to come and arrest Asher and I for burning down the property.

When I unlocked the door and opened it, the light from outside poured in. I couldn't see anything for a second as my eyes adjusted. "Can I help you?" I said in a tired voice.

"Tucker," a woman's voice spoke. She sounded relieved and overjoyed at the same time. There was a hint of something in her tone that I recognized immediately. And then, I saw her. My sister was standing in front of me.

"Tessa?" I murmured. I stood there in disbelief. Her face was just as beautiful as the day she left home. She looked slightly older with some new lines formed in her face, but those kind eyes were undeniable. Her hair was shorter than before and she wore older-looking clothes.

"Hi, Tuck," she smiled, tears forming in her eyes. She fidgeted with her hands as if she were nervous to be there, but that soon dissipated when I went to hug her. She wrapped her arms around me with all the love and sorrow we had both felt after being separated for so many years. We both broke down in tears. Our embrace was so overwhelming that we had to hold each other up to keep from crumbling to the ground in joy.

Tessa finally let go and placed her hands gently around my face to look at me. "Last time I saw you, you were tiny," she said through teary whimpers. She wrapped her arms around me once more, hugging me so tight as though she never wanted to let go.

I felt a wholeness in my heart that hadn't been there in a very long time.

When I looked up, I noticed Charli standing at the end of Asher's driveway with the biggest smile I had ever seen from her. As I let go of Tessa, I also realized that Asher was standing in the doorway, watching the moment.

"Are these your friends?" Tessa asked, keeping one arm around my shoulder.

"Uh, yeah," I wiped the tears from my face, "This is Asher and Charli. Guys, this is . . . my sister."

They both ran up excitedly to meet her. Technically, Asher had already met her as a kid, but it had been so long that he probably wouldn't have had a clue who she was. Without any hesitation, they embraced her like she was their family too.

It didn't take long for Tessa to realize how scratched up we were. "Oh my gosh!" she exclaimed, grabbing one of my arms to look at the marks. "Is this all from that fire?" she asked in a concerned, motherly manner. "The second I saw that on the news, I went straight to check up on you, Tuck. Mom and Dad said you'd be here."

The three of us gave each other knowing glances.

"It's a long story," I told her.

After we brought Tessa inside and explained the entirety of our October to her, she remained silent for a long time, deep in thought. We all hovered around the kitchen counter, waiting for someone to say something.

"You don't seem all that surprised," Charli spoke up.

Tessa shook her head with her hands intertwined in front of her mouth. "I'm not. I always knew there was something wrong with that place."

I looked at her in confusion. "What do you mean?"

"When I was a kid, I used to be friends with a girl named Evelyn Ross," Tessa said.

Asher and Charli turned to me immediately at the sound of that name.

"Ross? Like Cliff Ross?" Asher asked.

"Yeah," Tessa furrowed her brow, "How did you know?"

"Well, we were told that Cliff Ross was the previous

owner of the property and that he experienced all the weird stuff first," I explained.

Tessa nodded slowly. "Evelyn's his granddaughter. When we were kids, her parents would bring us there sometimes and that 'weird stuff' always happened. Evelyn hated going there. The last thing I heard about it before I left home was that the property was being sold. Evelyn told me she wanted to figure out what was actually happening at that place . . . but I haven't talked to her since. For all I know she could've moved away by now."

That was the end of our discussion for a while. Asher ordered pizza to the house and we let ourselves relax. Still running on empty stomachs from the night before, we devoured a whole box in minutes. Charli began to fall asleep on the couch while Asher quietly watched TV, giving Tessa and I some time to actually catch up on each other's lives.

"So, was the fire the only reason you came back?" I asked her, leaning against the counter.

A secretive grin spread across her face as she looked at me. She said nothing, but it was clear she wanted to. She was holding something back, something big.

"What?" I tilted my head curiously.

Her grin got even bigger. "Well, I was actually going to visit you soon anyway. Now that I have the money for it . . ." she veered off.

I folded my arms, my curiosity growing.

"I was thinking of buying a house . . . in Sleepy Hollow."

My jaw nearly hit the floor just by hearing her say that,

so you can imagine how unprepared I was for what came out of her mouth next.

"And I thought you might want to move in with me," her smile faded as she became apprehensive, "At least for a little while until you can get your own place. I don't know," she said, fidgeting with her hands. "I just thought you might want to escape our parents sooner than later."

I think my silence scared her but I had no idea what to say. It felt like my ability to form words was gone. Of course, I was going to say yes but all I could do for a solid minute was gawk at her while my heart became overjoyed.

She scrunched up her face anxiously. "So . . . what do you think?"

"Yeah," I nodded and shook my head at the same time, "I mean, of course I'll go with you. That's incredible, Tess."

"Really?" she said, breathing heavily with relief. "Okay. Great," she smiled.

God's timing is real. He was the only one who could've lined everything up so perfectly for me to reunite with my sister after all that had happened. It was perfect.

Just then, Asher stood up rapidly from the couch. "Hey, Tessa?" he called out.

"Yeah?" Tessa replied, instantly turning her head.

"Remember how you said that Evelyn wanted to find out what happened at the property? Well, I think she found out. Look," Asher said, turning up the volume on the TV.

The local news station was on and the headline read: **Farrington Property Fire: Arson or Accident?** The reporter on the screen was a woman around Tessa's age with dirty blonde hair and caked-on makeup. Her name was written in small white letters at the bottom of the screen.

"Evelyn Ross," Tessa murmured aloud.

Charli suddenly lifted her head at the sound of the TV. She looked up drearily and her eyes widened. "Wait, that's Evelyn. Like *that* Evelyn?" she pointed to the screen.

"Yeah, it's her. Welcome back," Asher said sarcastically. "Now shush." He turned the volume up a bit more.

Evelyn Ross's voice echoed through the speakers. "After a very long night for our firefighters, they were able to safely and successfully put the fire out on the property. Just this morning, the police completed a search of the premises after receiving numerous phone calls last night about missing persons. So far, 19 bodies have been found at various locations on the property, the majority of them residing in the woods. The police say they will not release any explicit details about the victims or their deaths, except that there may have been other factors involved other than the fire. There is still no clear explanation as to what caused the fire, but many believe that it was the owner herself: Shiloh Farrington. Authorities say they are going to continue the investigation until the truth about this gruesome phenomenon is revealed. That's all for now. Thanks for tuning in."

Weeks went by, and guess what, the authorities never found the truth they were looking for. Some of the missing people turned up, Jolene and Austin being two of them. We never heard anything about Abbie or Luke. We could only assume that they were a part of the 19 bodies that had been found. After a month, they closed the investigation. Nobody was ever even accused of being a suspect. It was like the police just gave up and wanted all the rumors of that property to finally die. But they didn't. People still talked about the whole thing, giving their crazy theories on social media, in interviews, at school; it was never-ending. All my friends and I could do was sit by and listen, despite how wrong everyone was. I didn't realize how much of a burden it was to carry such a weight on your shoulders and never be able to tell the world.

Eventually, I moved in with Tessa. She got a small house in a neighborhood near Asher and Charli's, that way we could still hang out whenever we wanted. They helped Tessa and I get settled in, and they would often stay the night. As time went on, we formed our own strange type of family, but it didn't feel that strange to me at all because I had always seen them as my family; it didn't matter if we were connected by blood or not.

Tessa and I both got jobs that would keep us stable for a long time. It was nice not having to worry about the possibility of falling into poverty at any random moment. Oh, and speaking of which, neither of us ever spoke to our parents again. As far as we were concerned, they were dead to us. It might sound sad, but it was better that way. We were happier.

I did my best to move on from what happened in those woods, we all did, but we knew it would never leave our minds. That October was a part of us for the rest of our lives. I felt such an incredible guilt from all of it. It hurt knowing that so many people died because of Metsah and that they were just food to her. But what hurt the most was knowing that I defended her for so long. I became a liar myself. At the time, I wholeheartedly wanted her to be good, to be better than the rest of them, but it was just never possible.

Now if I could give you all one last piece of advice, it would be to never trust the Devil. Ever.

~ 30 ~

SHILOH

It's been a while since any of you have heard from me, and you're probably surprised to even be hearing any of this now. No, I didn't somehow survive and get to tell my story. I am most certainly dead. Instead, God gave me the opportunity to share this with you while I was still on Earth, even with Metsah possessing my body. God showed me Metsah's future as a point of comfort and so I wrote all of this in one of Metsah's creation journals in hopes that it may reach someone. And it looks like it has. When I was strewn together with that woman's soul, it helped me to realize that my story wasn't for nothing. And by now you should all know my story down to the very last detail. You know that I was innocent, that it was Metsah who used me as a disguise for herself. She used me in the most unbearable ways and left the heaviest weight on my heart. Like the Devil, she is hated by everyone who knows her name. Although, if it were possible, I would've liked to have forgiven her. But unfortunately, it is very much impossible.

She bound her soul to an eternity of suffering and she has no one else to blame but herself. The Devil did not force her to do it, she did it all on her own volition simply because she was deprived of the life she wanted. Truthfully, there are many of us who are unsatisfied with the life we have, but that does not permit us to sell ourselves.

I had to watch from behind a curtain as Metsah killed those people. There was nothing I could do or say to stop her. I was powerless -- just a shadow in my own body. Their blood spilled at my feet, their hearts stopped in my hands, and their souls left their bodies right before my very eyes. I felt so worthless at the time. I couldn't understand why God was making me watch such horrible things or why He was even allowing Metsah to run amuck. But then I discovered Tucker and his friends. I realized that God was using Metsah to make all of them stronger. That's a lesson I wish everyone learned: when we don't understand why something is happening to us, we need to have the patience that lets us see God's plan take place. Or else we don't grow at all. We remain stubborn and closed off to the truth.

I won't sit here and complain that my life wasn't fair. I know it wasn't. And I know it's cliché when people say "life's not fair" but it's true. It is completely true. But as much as it hurts, it's necessary because it brings us closer to Him. If only Metsah had understood that when she was a little girl.

When I died in that fire, I felt so much relief. I was no longer trapped with all of the evil that was forced upon me. My soul flew up towards the eyes of the angels and before I knew it, I was home. There is no way for me to describe it to you except that I felt perfect happiness. No human on Earth knows that feeling, but I hope that someday you will. I hope that someday, you will join me in eternal peace and you will never have to see the faces of those who suffer like Metsah.

I beg all of you to learn from her. Trust me when I tell you that you do not want to embrace a life of agony and darkness as she did. Nothing good can come from it. In fact, she will continue to suffer. She is suffering right now. Those kids did not kill her; nobody ever has. They may have taken away her human form, but life runs far beyond our physical state. Some day, she will return through the tree that imprisoned her and her wrath will infect the Earth once more. It is only a matter of time.

-THE DEVIL CAN BE BEAUTIFUL, BUT BEAUTY CAN BE QUITE DECEIVING.

Cassie Hopwood is a high school student from Colorado. She had always dreamed of becoming an author as a child and she continued to write until she finally accomplished that dream. Her first published novel was Threat to the System: an action-packed, sci-fi story. She plans on writing more books until the day she dies.